Bolan pumped the brakes— nothing

He downshifted, slamming the lever into third. The roadster slowed enough for him to wrestle it around the curve, but another hairpin turn was dead ahead. He didn't have a hope of slowing the vehicle.

With a curse, the Executioner banged it into second and wrenched the wheel. Lurching, the Alfa ran off the road at the foot of the grade. As the tail swung out and struck the bank, the roadster burst through a stone parapet backward, rose into the air and somersaulted down the hillside in a shower of rocks.

Bolan had been thrown clear with the first impact. Bruised and shaken, he crouched behind a boulder, peering through the yellow dust cloud eddying up the slope.

Rock chips suddenly stung the warrior's cheek as a heavy-caliber slug whined off the boulder. Bolan was flat on his face behind the huge stone before the whipcrack of the power rifle high up on the escarpment reached his ears.

The Executioner had been betrayed.

MACK BOLAN®

The Executioner

#60 Sold for Slaughter
#61 Tiger War
#62 Day of Mourning
#63 The New War Book
#64 Dead Man Running
#65 Cambodia Clash
#66 Orbiting Omega
#67 Beirut Payback
#68 Prairie Fire
#69 Skysweeper
#70 Ice Cold Kill
#71 Blood Dues
#72 Hellbinder
#73 Appointment in Kabul
#74 Savannah Swingsaw
#75 The Bone Yard
#76 Teheran Wipeout
#77 Hollywood Hell
#78 Death Games
#79 Council of Kings
#80 Running Hot
#81 Shock Waves
#82 Hammerhead Reef
#83 Missouri Deathwatch
#84 Fastburn
#85 Sunscream
#86 Hell's Gate
#87 Hellfire Crusade
#88 Baltimore Trackdown
#89 Defenders and Believers
#90 Blood Heat Zero
#91 The Trial
#92 Moscow Massacre
#93 The Fire Eaters
#94 Save the Children
#95 Blood and Thunder
#96 Death Has a Name
#97 Meltdown
#98 Black Dice
#99 Code of Dishonor
#100 Blood Testament
#101 Eternal Triangle
#102 Split Image

#103 Assault on Rome
#104 Devil's Horn
#105 Countdown to Chaos
#106 Run to Ground
#107 American Nightmare
#108 Time to Kill
#109 Hong Kong Hit List
#110 Trojan Horse
#111 The Fiery Cross
#112 Blood of the Lion
#113 Vietnam Fallout
#114 Cold Judgment
#115 Circle of Steel
#116 The Killing Urge
#117 Vendetta in Venice
#118 Warrior's Revenge
#119 Line of Fire
#120 Border Sweep
#121 Twisted Path
#122 Desert Strike
#124 Night Kill
#125 Dead Man's Tale

Stony Man Doctrine
Terminal Velocity
Resurrection Day
Dirty War
Flight 741
Dead Easy
Sudden Death
Rogue Force
Tropic Heat
Fire in the Sky
Anvil of Hell
Flash Point
Flesh and Blood
Moving Target
War Born
Tightrope

DON PENDLETON's EXECUTIONER

MACK BOLAN.

Dead Man's Tale

A GOLD EAGLE BOOK FROM

WORLDWIDE.

TORONTO • NEW YORK • LONDON • PARIS
AMSTERDAM • STOCKHOLM • HAMBURG
ATHENS • MILAN • TOKYO • SYDNEY

First edition May 1989

ISBN 0-373-61125-0

Special thanks and acknowledgment to
Peter Leslie for his contribution to this work.

He who would greatly achieve must greatly dare, for brilliant victory is only achieved at the risk of disastrous defeat.

—Washington Irving, 1783-1859

My critics . . . want war too methodical, too measured; I would make it brisk, bold, impetuous, perhaps sometimes even audacious.

—Jomini: "Précis de l'Art de la Guerre", 1838

I refuse to stand idly by while the international Mob attempts worldwide consolidation. I'll hit fast and hard when they least expect it. And I'll take no prisoners in this war.

—Mack Bolan

THE
MACK BOLAN®
LEGEND

Nothing less than a war could have fashioned the destiny of the man called Mack Bolan. Bolan earned the Executioner title in the jungle hell of Vietnam.

But this soldier also wore another name—Sergeant Mercy. He was so tagged because of the compassion he showed to wounded comrades-in-arms and Vietnamese civilians.

Mack Bolan's second tour of duty ended prematurely when he was given emergency leave to return home and bury his family, victims of the Mob. Then he declared a one-man war against the Mafia.

He confronted the Families head-on from coast to coast, and soon a hope of victory began to appear. But Bolan had broken society's every rule. That same society started gunning for this elusive warrior—to no avail.

So Bolan was offered amnesty to work within the system against terrorism. This time, as an employee of Uncle Sam, Bolan became Colonel John Phoenix. With a command center at Stony Man Farm in Virginia, he and his new allies—Able Team and Phoenix Force—waged relentless war on a new adversary: the KGB.

But when his one true love, April Rose, died at the hands of the Soviet terror machine, Bolan severed all ties with Establishment authority.

Now, after a lengthy lone-wolf struggle and much soul-searching, the Executioner has agreed to enter an "arm's-length" alliance with his government once more, reserving the right to pursue personal missions in his Everlasting War.

PROLOGUE

For three hours the killers in the black Mercedes had been doing their damndest to close in on their prey. The agent's car, a small Peugeot convertible, was far less powerful, but it was more maneuverable and he could outaccelerate the heavy sedan in the hilly, wooded terrain.

That was fine—as long as he could steer clear of the flat country, as long as he could stay with the tourist traffic on these busy scenic routes. Each time he hit a straightaway, where the Mercedes could make use of its superior top speed, he was agonizingly aware of his vulnerability, of the target his broad back presented for the machine gunners in the sedan.

The American's own targets were simple: stay ahead of the killers long enough to make a large town; once there, lose them long enough to locate a post office and mail that vital package back to the States.

His goals were okay in theory, but the only town in the Grand Duchy of Luxembourg big enough to lose a professional tail was Luxembourg city itself. And to get there, forty kilometers to the south, he'd have to traverse, one way or another, the flatlands in the middle of the principality.

The killers had picked him up on the expressway east of Brussels, after he'd registered the photographic plates as air freight on a Sabena jetliner flying to New York. For security reasons he'd intended to send the second package by another route. Airmail it from Liège, perhaps. But the squat, dark bulk of the Mercedes, growing larger every second in his rearview mirror, had prompted him to leave the highway at the first opportunity and keep to the twisting side roads that penetrated the Ardennes.

He'd crossed into Luxembourg almost by accident, threading the little Peugeot through a network of secondary routes to avoid the long, straight, undulating, high-speed section that formed part of the Spa-Francorchamps racing circuit. Now he was near the town of Clervaux, in a part of the Grand Duchy known as Little Switzerland.

The track snaked across a ridge with panoramic views on either side, plunged into a crisscross of narrow, rock-walled valleys and finally tunneled through an evergreen forest to join the road that followed the course of the Clerf River.

Traffic was more dense here, where the highway, the river and the mainline railroad ran together along the floor of a sinuous gorge. The American tucked the Peugeot between two of the brightly painted trailers in a row of circus vehicles lumbering south. He knew that even if the gunmen in the Mercedes dared to pull out into the oncoming traffic to overtake him, they'd never shoot in front of so many witnesses. The sedan was registered in Palermo, Sicily, and the gunners would have orders to make one hundred percent certain that the hit was anonymous.

They wouldn't be sure of getting the package, either: with the driver dead, the convertible would most likely crash, perhaps go up in flames. Other drivers would stop and run over to see if they could help, preventing the mobsters from getting their hands on the goods.

Right now the hunted man was more worried about the white needle on his fuel gauge, which was hovering dangerously near the empty mark. There was a real danger that he could run out of gas before he made it to the capital.

Brakes squealed as the circus convoy slowed for an intersection. Swerving out from behind momentarily, the American saw traffic lights, a turnoff that led between tall, narrow old houses toward Diekirch, the vineyards of the Moselle Valley and the German frontier.

The convoy swung left and took the road for Diekirch.

The American swore. He slammed the stick shift into second and shot a red light. The convertible laid down rubber, wheels spinning as he arrowed it between the stalls of a street market.

In the rearview mirror, he saw a panel truck, a BMW, then the black Mercedes. At the far end of the street was a signboard that read: Luxembourg 25.

Almost exactly fifteen miles.

The town of Wiltz was long gone. He had to be near Ettelbruck. And between there and Mersch, the road ran across a flat countryside punctuated by isolated farms, with few trees, no woods and scarcely a curve for the next seven miles....

The panel truck stopped outside a shed stacked with lumber. Two hundred meters farther on, the BMW turned in through the white gates of a large house. The American was alone with the killers.

There was nothing he could do but press on and await the inevitable. He was unarmed: his .38-caliber Police Special had been taken when they ransacked his hotel room in Brussels and stole back the originals of the photocopied sheets he'd delivered to Sabena at the airport.

He reckoned they knew about the photographs. Otherwise they wouldn't be so determined to eliminate him and grab the second package, without which the photo plates would be useless.

Two miles out from Ettelbruck, the gunners opened fire for the first time.

The road climbed out of a shallow valley and ran straight ahead for a kilometer before it vanished over a slight rise. There was no traffic in either direction, a tiny chapel was the only building visible among fields of sugar beet, maize and yellow mustard.

The tuned engine of the Peugeot howled as the American held the pedal flat against the floor. But slowly the Mercedes gained. When it was twenty meters away, the tinted electric window on the passenger side slid down, and the modular snout and grooved handgrip of a Heckler & Koch MP-5 submachine gun appeared. Flame danced briefly around the muzzle.

The weapon was silenced. The American heard nothing over the rasp of the little car's exhaust. The first he knew of the attack was a searing pain that ripped across the top of his right shoulder. The windshield starred and became opaque.

The driver smashed his fist through the safety glass, punching out a hole to see through as the convertible veered wildly across the road.

Engine straining, the Mercedes closed meter by meter. After that first short ranging volley, the gunner took longer over the second burst. The American felt the car shudder as a stream of subsonic 9 mm slugs thudded into the bodywork beneath the folded top.

He cursed again. He was unfamiliar with the car; he'd rented it from an agency at the airport outside Brussels. Where was the gas tank? Were the bastards aiming for it? Gritting his teeth, he began to swerve the Peugeot across the road, blocking any attempt by the sedan to draw alongside.

The gunman was leaning out the window now. He leveled the SMG and fired again. Fiberglass chips and bright fragments of metal bounced and spun across the pavement behind the convertible. And this time there could be no doubt about it: wind screaming through the hole in the smashed windshield was creating a turbulence in the back of the car that forced the sweet, acrid odor of gasoline forward, washing it over the driver.

He squinted his eyes half-closed against the airflow buffeting his face. He punched more glass from the shattered windshield, wincing with pain as the effort sent fire flaming through the shoulder. He thought the wound was superficial, a furrow gouged along the side of his neck, because he could still use his arm, and the blood, warm on his flesh, was congealing before it reached his wrist. It hurt like hell, just the same, each time he moved.

The rearview mirror was still intact. He swerved the Peugeot again and saw the image of the gunman reappear at the window of the sedan. But this time no flame flickered from the SMG. The killer had exhausted the clip.

As the gunner slumped back into his seat to reload, the Peugeot breasted the rise and raced down the long, straight downgrade on the far side. Three car-lengths behind, the driver of the Mercedes swung wide to draw level...and then pulled the sedan back as a semitrailer labored around a curve and began to lumber up the hill toward them.

Two hundreds meters ahead, a tractor pulling a cart heavily laden with bales of hay had turned out of a dirt road and blocked the way. Brakes screeching, the convertible left black rubber on the pavement as it skidded sideways to avoid the slow-moving load.

Then, shifting down with a yell of protest from the engine, the American squeezed the car through the narrowing gap between the bales of hay and the advancing semi, rocketing on toward the curve at the foot of the grade.

The driver of the Mercedes couldn't make it. He stood on the pedal, heaving up on the hand brake at the same time. Then, at the last moment, feeling the sedan start to break away, he released the brakes and shot across in front of the semi onto the grass bordering the road.

Clumps of earth flew into the air; big wheels plowed furrows among the wayside blossoms; the front fender of the Mercedes scarred a bank beneath a hedgerow. Then the vehicle bumped back onto the road.

The Peugeot convertible was three hundred meters ahead now, preparing to take the curve. A short distance beyond, a stand of trees shaded the entrance to a village.

The American's breath quickened. Did he have a chance after all? He dared to hope.

Seconds later, Fate dealt him a joker, and he rethought the whole deal.

The village was a single long street with stores lining both sides. Halfway down the street, a file of country folk clambered aboard a bus, a green-and-cream vehicle with a plume of diesel smoke fanning from the tail pipe. The word Luxembourg was lettered in white on its side.

The American shot past the bus and brought the Peugeot to a halt by the sidewalk. He snatched a black leather satchel from among the glass fragments littering the passenger seat and ran back to the bus. He squeezed on board just as the hydraulic doors hissed shut.

The bus driver took his money and punched out a ticket. He shifted into Drive and the bus lurched forward.

Panting, the hunted man clamped the satchel beneath his injured arm, clasped his left hand over the blood-stain on his shoulder and sank into a vacant seat.

Through the rear window, he saw the Mercedes pull in behind.

It remained there, sometimes crawling immediately behind, sometimes separated by a truck or a few cars. And then, turning around when the bus started to grind up a steep grade, the American noticed that the sedan was no longer with them. The killers and their car had apparently abandoned the chase.

He shrugged. He would have to be especially watchful when he left the bus, that was all.

But there was no black Mercedes sedan to be seen when he got off the bus in the city center. No suspicious characters jostled him as he moved among the late-afternoon shoppers crowding the sidewalks as he made his way to the post office. The broad flight of steps leading up to the entrance was deserted. He took them three at a time.

The sniper—alerted by the killers in the Mercedes—drilled a precision round through the American's temple. He never knew what hit him.

1

It was the slickest snatch Washington had experienced in years.

At 10:16 a.m. Mack Bolan, a.k.a. the Executioner, turned a handle and walked through a doorway that led to the D.C. safehouse of Hal Brognola's Sensitive Operations Group. At 10:17 Bolan was lying unconscious on the floor of a car heading south for the Capitol Beltway.

The morning was sunny, with high white clouds sailing lazily across a clear sky. It had been raining earlier, but by the time Bolan paid off his cab on Eleventh Street, the sidewalks had steamed themselves dry and the tires of traffic streaming down from Capitol Hill no longer hissed over the patched pavement. Hal Brognola, boss of the group and its sole link with the White House, was due to take off for some well-earned R and R. And although the big Fed used the place as a safehouse when he needed to meet illegals whose presence at his Justice Department office would have been an embarrassment, Bolan's business at the HQ involved nothing more lethal than to make arrangements to meet Brognola for a backpacking trip into the Blue Ridge Mountains. Five minutes after he had paid off the cab, he entered a corner grocery store at the end of a line of redbrick town houses.

A nondescript Plymouth was maneuvering into a gap between two vehicles parked at the side of the road as he pushed open the door. Behind the reflection of his own dark hair, blue eyes and hawklike features, a section of the sunny street slanted away and swung inward as the glass-paneled door opened.

In the street behind him, a wino with a stogie drooping from his unshaven lip put a hand on the arm of a passing businessman in an unspoken request for a light. The digital clock above the newsstand read 10:16.

Bolan walked into the store and proceeded immediately to the back, where two phone booths stood. He entered the left-hand booth, which was half hidden by a rack of paperback whodunnits, and lifted the handset of an old dial telephone. Then, reading the figures off a line penciled on a slip of paper, he spun out the nine-digit code for that day.

While waiting for the secret door at the back of the booth to slide open, Bolan glanced into the store. Nick Alexiou, the elderly Greek who ran the business, was in his shirt-sleeves, crouched over a desk in the shadows at the far end of the long, narrow room. A blonde Bolan hadn't seen before sat behind the cash register.

The girl looked at Alexiou and made eye contact, favoring him with a lopsided smile. The old man grunted something unintelligible and hunched himself still farther over his paperwork.

Interpreting the gesture as Alexiou being in one of his irascible moods, the Executioner shrugged, cocked an approving eye at the curves beneath the coveralls and turned back to the phone.

Beyond the sliding door, a passageway led to a house in the next block, a villa with white-painted bay windows, its yard bright with spring flowers. Indoors, the villa was not quite what it seemed to folks strolling along the quiet residential street. Closed circuit cameras mon-

itored every square foot of the building. Alarm sensors
protected each opening in the armored walls, and bulletproof steel shutters could seal off doors and windows at
the touch of a switch. A sophisticated, electronically
shielded computer complex was stationed next to Brognola's second-floor office.

A severe-looking woman wearing thick glasses sat behind the desk in the reception area that filled the villa's
hallway. She'd seen Bolan's arrival at the grocery store on
the monitor linked to the camera in the phone booth.
Once she'd checked the number he dialed against an entry in a code book, she pressed the button that would
deactivate the locking magnets and allow hydraulic rams
to slide open the secret door.

The door didn't open.

Normally, conditioned by long training and by years of
combat in the field, Bolan's catlike alertness never relaxed. Even when he wasn't on a mission.

Today, however—perhaps relaxed and amused by the
thought of a hike through the woods with his out-of-
shape friend—he must have been fractionally less vigi-
lant than usual.

Which was why several seconds elapsed before he realized that the correctly dialed code was *not* opening the
door, and that a faint but persistent hissing above his
head was connected with an unexpected odor in the air.

Bolan's reflexes snapped abruptly back into top gear.
He noticed the narrow, deep cuts in the woodwork that
must have severed the electric circuit that controlled the
door mechanism, saw the tiny cylinder of gas hidden in
the dead area just below the lens of the video camera.
And saw, too, the deft arrangement of fine wires through
which, by spinning the dial, he had triggered the release
of the cylinder's contents.

Desperately he stretched up toward the container and its deadly gas, but his arms seemed abnormally heavy, his fingers thick and numb. A loud noise thundered in his ears, and his chest was on fire. Whirling, he ran for the door through which he'd entered, and the lifegiving fresh air beyond—at least that was what his fogged brain commanded his muscles to do. All he achieved was a staggering half turn as he slumped against the wall of the booth....

The man masquerading as Alexiou nodded to his blond companion. Together they dragged the Executioner toward the door, hauling him by the legs as though they were the handles of a wheelbarrow. They were joined by two men—a businessman in a dark suit and a Homberg hat and an unsavory-looking character with stubble on his chin. The four picked up the unconscious warrior and stood just inside the open door of the shop in a compact group, supporting Bolan's body between them.

Somebody signaled from the front seat of the Plymouth and opened the rear door.

Swiftly the ill-assorted quartet ferried Bolan across the flagstones and shoved him through the open door feet first. The blonde leaned inside the sedan and pulled a lever. The seat back hinged forward to reveal a dark cavity. There was a concerted heave, and Bolan disappeared from view.

As the seat swung into position again, the blonde and the man from the store climbed into the car and closed the door. The businessman and his companion unhurriedly crossed the road and mingled with the few pedestrians on the far side. Equally unhurried, the Plymouth nosed out into the traffic and drove away.

The figures on the clock above the newsstand flashed off and on again: 10:17. The snatch had taken fifty-seven seconds.

Passersby who had noticed what had transpired were still staring as the Plymouth drove through the intersection. And by the time the receptionist in Brognola's villa had come to her senses and stabbed the alarm button, the getaway car had vanished in the swirl of midmorning city traffic.

2

Hal Brognola threw an unlit Willem II onto the stack of reports in the center of his desk. "Why?" he exploded, spreading his arms wide in exasperation. "I just can't understand why someone would grab Bolan at this point in time."

The cigar teetered on the edge of a buff folder, tipped over and rolled across the polished wood to come to rest precisely opposite its reflection. Frank O'Reilly, the fifty-year-old ex-FBI agent responsible for internal security, stared out the window at the sunlight dappling an acacia tree. "You say he wasn't involved in a mission?" he queried.

"Bolan's not on the team," the Fed snapped irritably. "You know that, Frank. Strictly speaking, he never is on a mission, not from us. As far as I know, he wasn't following up on any of his own interests. We were going backpacking, for God's sake!"

O'Reilly sighed. "Then if there's no lead, motivewise, all we can do is collect everything we can on the kidnapping itself, however insignificant, and work from there."

"Nothing is insignificant where Striker's concerned," Brognola growled. "You can have as many men as you want. Any help you need from the FBI, the Company, Interpol, the local police department. Just ask." The big man was shaken by the drama. "Grabbed on our own doorstep?" he muttered, rubbing a hand over his face. "It's almost indecent."

"You didn't actually give me the kidnappers' MO yet," O'Reilly reminded him gently.

"What happened? Somebody tricked the kid who handles Alexiou's deliveries into going to an uptown apartment block with a load of groceries. Of course it was a decoy call. Nobody at that address had ordered anything. While the kid was away, they came to the store, abducted the old man and put in a ringer, someone sufficiently like him to fool Bolan from the shadows in back of the store. There was a girl, too. A blonde in white coveralls."

The security man frowned. "None of our own people coming in and out noticed anything?"

"According to the reports, it was brilliantly timed." Brognola picked out a paper from the top folder. "Yeah...Zimmerman went out at 9:49. Alexiou and the kid were both there then, definitely. He talked with them. Montefiori came in at 10:02, and he's fairly sure the old man was there, though he didn't notice the assistant. In any case, the sliding door in the booth must have been working because he used it. Yet by the time Bolan arrived fourteen minutes later, at 10:16, the substitution had been made and the trap set. They must have moved the moment Montefiori was through."

"How did they actually fix it, sir?"

"They were smart enough. A small gas canister lodged beneath the lens of the monitor camera. The door controls were cut. When Bolan dialed, he pulled a wire tripping a plunger that pierced the nozzle of the cylinder and released the stuff. End of story."

"End of...? You don't mean—"

"No, no. According to our lab technicians, it was a nerve gas that would only knock him out for a couple of hours, that's all."

"So they must want him for some specific purpose." O'Reilly looked relieved. "There's something that bugs me, just the same. Even if the canister was out of TV range, why didn't the receptionist see them fixing it? They must have been in camera range the whole time."

"That's something we're looking into right now," the Fed replied grimly. He pressed a button and spoke into an intercom. "Send in Miss Haslett and the lieutenant."

The shortsighted receptionist was accompanied by a thickset man with a crew cut. "Lieutenant Benito," the Fed announced.

O'Reilly nodded. The policeman, who had high security clearance, was from the local police station. He turned his glowering regard on the woman, who had obviously been crying. "I can't imagine," he said furiously, "how you failed to give the alarm earlier."

Brognola looked expectantly at the receptionist.

"I didn't know," Miss Haslett burst out. "I *was* watching the monitor. I saw Mr. Bolan come in and start to dial. Then he seemed to... well, sort of stagger. I thought he'd been taken ill suddenly. Then Mr. Alexiou ran to help him—at least, I thought it was Mr. Alexiou—with a woman in white coveralls."

"Well?"

Miss Haslett hesitated, staring at the edge of Brognola's desk. "I figured it was a nurse. I would have reported it later, of course, but I never thought of sounding the alarm. They took him back into the store, and then it hit me that nurses aren't already there when a person falls ill. You have to send for them. So I sounded the alarm, but of course by then it was too late. I feel so foolish." The woman was weeping again, the tears coursing down her face and streaking her cheeks with mascara.

"That is possibly understandable—if not forgivable in an employee holding a position of trust," Brognola said sternly. "What we want to know about is the previous foul-up."

"The previous . . . ?"

"Miss Haslett!" He glared. "A device was rigged in that booth. It was intended to render Bolan unconscious, and it succeeded. But it must have taken several minutes to set up. During that time the persons engaged in the operation must have been in full view of the monitor camera, which you, supposedly, were watching. Would you mind explaining how you failed to see that?"

The receptionist swallowed. "I guess it must have been just a little while before?"

"It was," Brognola rasped. "Between 10:03 and 10:15."

"Yes, sir. Well, I saw Mr. Alexiou—the man I *thought* was Mr. Alexiou—come into the booth. I was aware that he was doing something there. I could see him out of the corner of my eye—"

"Out of the corner of your eye!" O'Reilly shouted. "You're employed to *watch* those fucking monitors."

"I know, sir. But there was this other commotion that I was watching on number three."

"Commotion?" Brognola echoed. "What commotion?"

"Some guy tried to force his way in through the personnel entrance behind the carport," O'Reilly told him. "When they wouldn't let him by, he got violent and tried to start a fight. I went there myself to sort it out."

Brognola sighed. "Classic diversionary tactic on the opposite flank. There's been some planning here. Why wasn't I told of this before?"

"It's all in the reports, sir. On your desk."

"Reports, reports!" Brognola stirred the papers with a contemptuous forefinger. "What I want is action. The man who staged this decoy routine—you let him go, I suppose?"

"I'm afraid so, sir. Threatened to arrest him for trespassing and threw him out. It's standard procedure. Of course, if we'd known..."

Brognola growled something unintelligible, then shot the woman from Reception a sudden glance from under his eyebrows. "You know what this means?" he said gruffly.

She nodded her head. "I understand, sir," she replied in a low voice. "And I'm sorry."

"So am I, Miss Haslett, so am I. You better go wait outside in case Mr. O'Reilly or the lieutenant have any more questions."

"What do you think?" the policeman asked when the sobbing woman had left. "You know your staff. Was she in on the deal? Did someone get to her, persuade her to take a bribe, look the wrong way for five minutes?"

"Search me," Brognola replied. "I'm inclined to think not. The screening here is tough. But we have to let her go. That's standard procedure, too. We can't afford to take chances. And even if we had time to check it out, you can never be a hundred percent sure of anyone after a thing like that. Not one hundred percent. What leads do you have, Lieutenant?"

The cop looked at the floor. "Not too many, to tell you the truth. Four people carried your man to the car, according to an eyewitness. Must have been a second couple hanging around outside the store, I'd say."

"How many eyewitnesses?"

"Just the one—as far as the actual snatch is concerned. A middle-aged woman on her way to the supermarket. At least, she's the only one to come forward. There must have been others, a sunny morning like this, but we haven't located them yet."

"She got a good view of the kidnappers?"

"Yeah, but the descriptions aren't worth a damn. Blond girl in white coveralls, a silver-haired guy in his shirt-sleeves, a city gentleman dressed to kill and a bum. Could be thousands answering those descriptions in this one precinct."

Brognola compressed his lips. The lines on his tired face seemed to have etched themselves in more deeply. "Guess you're right. What about the car? She notice that?"

"Not really. She thought there were two guys—two other guys, that is—in the front seat. But that's all she could say. The boys are having her go over it all again down at the station. We do have another witness, though, to the car itself—from the other side of the street."

"Who? They see the snatch as well as the car?"

Benito pulled a notebook from his breast pocket, opened it, and flicked his eyes over the penciled notes. "Whetnall, Randy Whetnall. He's about fifty, fifty-five, and runs the newsstand right across the street. He didn't see anything of the kidnapping, but he noticed the car, because it was hovering there as if the driver was trying to make up his mind whether to park by a fire hydrant, and he knew the policeman was due any minute."

"The patrolman notice the car?"

"Yes, sir, he did. And his description tallies with Whetnall's—as far as it goes. But he was too far away to see much. He was hurrying to slap a ticket on them when they pulled away."

"And the car?"

The lieutenant spread his arms helplessly and shrugged. "One of the family heaps you don't notice. Eighty-six Plymouth Sundance. Or it might have been a Dodge. A pale color—light blue, gray, tan. Maybe a silver that had gotten very dusty, Whetnall thought. But what's the point? With that kind of car, you lose it the moment it's past the first intersection. Not a chance. We'll try, of course, but..." He shrugged again as his voice tailed away.

"I'm leaving the outside angle to you, Lieutenant," Brognola cut in. "You're better equipped for it than we are. But since you don't hold out much hope of identifying the vehicle, which might have been stolen anyway, I imagine the best lead has to come from the snatch itself. We'll take care of things inside the building—the Reception affair, checking on who knew Bolan was coming, the diversion in back, and so on. O'Reilly here is in charge of the operation. I suggest you keep an open line between his office and the squad room."

"Okay," the lieutenant agreed. "But what do you say we talk again with Whetnall for starters? We let him stay at his stand instead of taking him downtown. There's nobody to cover for him, and he can't afford to lose the business."

The security chief nodded. "We're on our way," he told Brognola.

Outside the grocery store, O'Reilly and the lieutenant stood at the edge of the sidewalk waiting for a gap in the lunchtime traffic so that they could cross the street. Benito waved cheerily to the news vendor. Whetnall, two hundred and forty pounds of blue-chinned geniality sweating in the sun, shouted back some ribald reply as he flourished a bottle he had produced from under the counter.

"He's a character," Benito said with a crooked smile. "We can make it now... No! Hold it! Those goddamn cabdrivers!"

"This time," O'Reilly urged. "Before that truck— *Christ! Look out!*"

Automobiles, cabs, trucks, buildings whirled abruptly as the cop spun to the pavement, propelled by a violent push between his shoulder blades. The concussive force of an explosion had thrown him to the ground.

O'Reilly levered himself to his knees and the palms of his hands, shaking his head to clear his vision. "Too late," he panted. "Too late, dammit, by the width of a street!" Scowling, he stared after the car from which the bomb had been thrown—a pale-colored nondescript sedan hurtling toward the lights at the intersection.

As the lights flashed from green to red, the sedan swerved out from behind a truck, pulled over to the left-hand side of the street and roared past the line of slowing cars to make the junction across the surge of oncoming traffic. They heard the squeal of its tires as it lurched into a side street beyond the lights.

The lieutenant was staring at the opposite sidewalk. "As far as we're concerned," he said shakily, "I'd say it was too *early* by the width of a street!"

Through the dust, the splintered remains of the newsstand pierced the air like the spars of a sinking ship. Above the glass that littered the flagstones, thousands of pinups from Whetnall's girlie magazines, ripped by the explosion, were fluttering down through the spring sunshine like the leaves of some unseasonal autumn. There was a great deal of blood.

But of the man with the bottle, the witness who might have been able to furnish some more definite intel on the car in which the Executioner had been abducted, nothing recognizable remained.

A patrolman ran up and helped Benito to his feet. "Message from Laforge at the station, Lieutenant," he gasped. "They found the body of a man stuffed into a trash can in an alley two blocks from here. He'd been garroted with a length of piano wire—a Greek storekeeper by the name of Alexiou."

3

The atmosphere in the safehouse was gloomy. O'Reilly and Lieutenant Benito sat on one side of Brognola's big desk while the Fed paced up and down on the other.

"A kidnapping and two murders in one morning!" he barked. "Nothing personal, Frank, but after a three-strike situation of that kind you begin to doubt the efficiency of the whole damned organization. This is just too much!"

After an uncomfortable silence Benito cleared his throat. "Still no word from the other side?" he queried. "No threatening calls, no ransom notes, no attempts to bargain?"

"None. And there won't be now. In my book," Brognola said, "kidnappers who want to use the hostage as a bargaining tool usually make their play almost at once, while relatives or associates are still in a state of shock."

"So why grab him?" O'Reilly objected. "If nobody is asking for money or some kind of favor against his safe return, what could be the point?"

Brognola looked at Benito. "Lieutenant, you don't know Bolan, how about giving us an objective rundown."

"Abductions," Benito said, "and the hostage situations that follow, customarily arise for one of five reasons." He ticked them off on his fingers. "One, to make the victim talk; two, to stop him talking; three, to make him do something or stop him doing something; four, to prevent someone who values him doing something; and five, to persuade someone to do something they wouldn't normally do—hand over money, release prisoners or whatever."

Brognola slumped into his swivel chair. "And so?"

"Since your Mr. Bolan isn't on assignment, I guess we can discount the second, third and fourth. So we are left with the supposition that his capture is to act as a lever, as a means to blackmail you into some course of action—"

"No way," Brognola interrupted, shaking his head decisively. "I told you he's not part of the team. He's a loner. He's also a friend, but nothing that happened to him could in the slightest way affect the policy of the group."

"Or," Benito continued, "they snatched him because they want the opportunity to make him talk."

"Bolan?" O'Reilly interjected. "About what?"

The policeman shrugged. "You tell me. Details of the antiterrorist or crime-busting techniques being developed by organizations he's in contact with. Maybe something like that."

"It's possible," the Fed conceded.

Benito said, "Coming back, sir, to the mechanics of the kidnapping. There are a couple more questions I'd like answered."

"I'm listening, Lieutenant."

"Okay. Now, as far as exits and entrances go, the kidnappers must have been familiar with your security setup."

"Intimately."

"And doesn't that suggest an inside accomplice to you?"

"Not necessarily. You're thinking of Susan Haslett, of course. Although we keep a low profile here, we do have visitors, you know. Army officers. Police officials from several countries. Operatives sometimes from the FBI, the CIA, Britain's MI-6 or even the French DGSE intelligence service. Any of them could piece together enough to plan the kidnapping and the diversion preceding it, once they'd been here a few times. It's not beyond the bounds of possibility that one of the less reputable intelligence agencies could kidnap a man like Bolan if they figured he had intel that could help them best an adversary."

"Hell," O'Reilly put in, "all they needed to know was the fact that contacts entered through Alexiou's store, that there was another entrance in back of the villa and that a single person monitored the closed circuit TV covering the whole complex. They could have learned details of how the door in the phone booth worked by becoming customers—once they knew there was something to look for."

"That's true," Brognola agreed. "After all, they didn't know, or need to know, the access code. Their aim was to *stop* the door from opening." He paused as the buzzer on the intercom sounded. "Yes? What is it? I particularly asked not to be disturbed."

"I'm very sorry to interrupt, Mr. Brognola," a woman's voice, "but the police station is calling Lieutenant Benito. They said it was urgent."

"Oh, very well. Lieutenant, take it at my desk."

As the policeman picked up the receiver, Brognola rose to his feet and moved over to join O'Reilly. "All this drama," he growled. "Has Zulowski reported?"

"Has he ever!" The security chief was suddenly enthusiastic. "He's come up with something better than we hoped for. He got the list!"

"You're kidding!" Brognola's rumpled features revealed his incredulity. "I never thought he'd pull it off. Are you, uh, you're certain the list's authentic?"

"No doubt at all. He got it from Mr. Big's safe in Cologne."

"They know we have it, of course?"

"Sure they do. Know we *had* it, that is. After he cracked the safe, they were on to him before he made it back across the frontier into Belgium. They repossessed it too, stole it from his hotel room in Brussels. But he'd already photographed each page and forwarded the negs to us."

"Great. When do we get the pictures?"

"I'll know tonight when he makes his routine report. His daily transmission was fading, and died before he could tell me."

"We'll probably receive them through the usual channels tomorrow or the day after. Microdot, I guess."

"Not this time. Zulowski was using a new technique. He told me that he was..."

O'Reilly's voice tailed off as Benito replaced the receiver. The policeman's face was white.

"That was my captain," he said tightly. "The people we're dealing with are ruthless, all right. Our female witness...she was having a cup of coffee with the boys in the squad room, and they got her. In there."

"My God!" Brognola's face blanched. "How?"

"A sniper on the roof of an apartment building right across the street. He drilled her through the head. She died instantly."

There was a short silence. "So," Brognola said at last, "since Whetnall and Alexiou are dead, and the delivery kid can't tell us anything, we're back to square one. Without a single lead to follow."

"Not quite," Benito ventured. "The getaway car, or one just like it, has been traced. A pale gray Plymouth has been found abandoned on the perimeter of a private airfield fifteen miles south of Alexandria. The forensic boys are still working on it, but they already found a special compartment between the rear seat and the trunk where they think your man must have been hidden while he was driven up there."

"And the flights out of that field since this morning?"

"Rookie pilots doing circuits and bumps, a couple of club members on dual with their instructors, some big wheel from GM on his way to Detroit—" Benito paused for effect "—and a Cessna executive jet that took off at a quarter to twelve without permission from the tower or the area controller, and without filing a flight plan."

"That's our man!" Brognola cried. "And the plane? What have they—"

"Rented from an agency at Moorestown field, in Burlington County, Philadelphia," the policeman cut in, "by a guy with all the right papers, professional jet pilot, cash on the nail. We have the names of course, but with an operation this professional they're bound to be phony."

Brognola was plucking at his lower lip. "Professional is right. And jet transport spells a big deal to me, and a long-term one. With enemies this well organized, well enough informed to plan the kidnap from our own base and eliminate witnesses the way they did, I'd say they *knew* Bolan was between missions."

He shuffled the papers on the desk for a moment, patting the edges to line them up in a neat pile, then he added, "And in view of the other deductions we've made, that leaves us with one inescapable conclusion. Bolan has been abducted at this particular time precisely *because* he's not involved in a mission. And you can make of that just what you like."

"Just a minute!"

Benito had been pacing, but stopped abruptly. "The description of the guy who rented the Cessna tallies with that of the ringer who sat in for Alexiou. And we do have a witness who saw *him*."

O'Reilly dived for the intercom, stabbing the button down. "Monica? Has Miss Haslett left the building?"

"Yes, Mr. O'Reilly, you just missed her," the woman replied. "She left a couple minutes ago. She, well, she seemed kind of upset."

The security chief was out the door and down the stairs in a flash. He ran out into the villa's front yard. A gate in a white picket fence stood open at the far end of the stone pathway. A tall hedge screened the yard from the street.

O'Reilly saw the thick-lensed glasses first. They lay on the path just inside the gateway. He swung around toward the hedge. Dentures grinned up at him from the trampled earth beneath a laurel, and beyond them he saw leaves from a broken branch and a single high-heeled shoe.

Susan Haslett lay five yards away. A blackened tongue protruded from her drawn-back lips, and her lifeless eyes bulged grotesquely. The looped wire of the garrote was buried almost out of sight in the swollen, empurpled flesh of her neck.

4

Yeah, it was the only possible answer, Mack Bolan thought. He must have been snatched because he was *not* on a mission. But why? What were his captors hoping to get out of it? He wasn't familiar with the long-range plans for Brognola's teams and he had no connection with anyone at Langley. So what was the point?

For the hundredth time he shook his head in puzzlement. His reasoning had followed exactly the same lines as Brognola's, and he had arrived at the same conclusion. The Executioner, however, had more impressions, more facts to go on—even though they didn't take him any nearer the solution of the mystery.

He remembered vividly his surprise when he heard the hiss of escaping gas, recalled his fury when his drugged muscles refused to obey the commands of his brain. After that there was a timeless blank broken only by sensations of movement. Once he had a confused idea that he'd been awakened from a deep sleep. He sensed pressure on his eardrum, a roaring all around him. Then cold fingers had pinched a fold of flesh on his arm and there had been a stinging sensation before he fell asleep again.

He could see the marks of the hypodermic now, just in the bend of the elbow. There were three punctures, and the joint was still painful. After that he remembered nothing at all until he came to in bed.

But there were plenty of impressions to mull over since that initial return to consciousness. He had sat up then in the unfamiliar room, hearing nothing but the slow pounding of blood through his own veins. He was wearing pajamas, and there were silk sheets on the bed. The room was wallpapered with crimson damask. His clothes, neatly pressed, were laid out on one of the petit point chairs. It looked like the bridal suite of a very expensive nineteenth-century hotel, or the guest room of an oilman's Park Avenue house.

Bolan swung his feet to the floor and stood. Other than a slight dizziness, there seemed to be nothing wrong with him.

Experimentally he walked across the Aubusson carpet to the window. A tug at the broad, tasseled cord hanging to one side soundlessly drew back the heavy velvet draperies. Outside it was daylight, with bright sunshine splashing the shadows of poplar trees across a lawn below.

He tried the bedroom door. Astonishingly it was unlocked. A wide corridor hung with modernistic paintings led to a gallery that encircled a huge entrance hall.

Hastily drawing on his clothes, Bolan softfooted out and down the shallow staircase to the ground floor. Once he had walked a few paces, the lightheadedness vanished. Through double glass doors at the far end of the hallway he could glimpse formal gardens that stretched away to a stand of trees.

He'd seen nobody and heard nothing. Feeling like a man in a dream, he walked out the doors onto a flagged terrace bordered by scarlet geraniums in urns.

The place was enormous—a rambling two-story house covered with vines; stables and a coach house; a servants' wing with kitchen gardens attached; rose gardens, sunken gardens, a topiary around an Olympic-size pool. Beyond a lawn fringed with cedars he came to a sweep of parkland. At the far side of this, a high wall marked the boundary of the property.

And ten yards inside this wall was a six-foot chain-link fence beaded at intervals with green glass insulators.

The ground between the fence and the wall had been cleared, and two large Doberman pinschers halted their patrol to stare coldly at him with baleful brown eyes.

Fifty yards farther, Bolan came suddenly on a man in a brown suit and pointed, two-tone shoes who was leaning against the trunk of a tree. There was a matchstick between his teeth, and cradled negligently in his arms was an Ingram submachine gun fitted with a MAC suppressor.

"Hi," Bolan said, affecting innocent friendliness. "It seems I'm a prisoner here. Do you know why?"

The eyes in the gunman's sallow face were hidden by shades. He shifted the weapon to a more comfortable position in the crook of his arm, removed the match with his other hand and spit. He neither looked at the Executioner nor replied to his question.

The warrior shrugged nonchalantly and turned back toward the house. He reckoned the property covered thirty acres. As he walked the perimeter, he saw several more pairs of dogs between the wire and the wall. And enough guards to make sure there wasn't a single yard that wasn't covered by at least one of them.

When upstairs in the bedroom again, he reviewed the situation mentally. He'd been grabbed in a fast, well-planned raid. He'd been brought to this place, and clearly the kidnappers meant to keep him here. For he was under no illusions—despite the unlocked bedroom door, the relaxed atmosphere of monied ease and the lack of direct surveillance, any attempt to escape would mean his death as surely as if he had stepped in front of a firing squad.

The fence, the dogs, the silent gunners all proved that. They proved too that whoever had masterminded the grab was a big time operator indeed....

So why should such a person want him here? No doubt he would find out soon enough, when the crunch came. For this was a prison, even though the bars weren't always visible. Meanwhile... where was he?

Once again he looked out the window. The sun was sinking. Beyond the wall, lush silvery meadows stretched into a distance barred at intervals with hedges and trees. Here and there in the hollows he could see patches of dogwood, and there were two farms—low buildings in mellow, rose-colored brick surrounded by poplars. Far away, a range of hills smudged an uneven line against the pale sky. No urban development could be seen on either side of the house.

It was a scene familiar and yet in some way entirely alien.

Where could they have brought him? Presumably, if they had really flown, it must be some distance from Washington. Could it Vermont? Southern Ohio? Wisconsin?

He shook his head. It could have been, but somehow he was sure it wasn't. Yet it certainly wasn't a landscape from anywhere near the Coast or even the South. He gazed out over the pastoral scene, seeking some clue among the fields and woods drowsing in the dusk.

"Do you prefer places to people, Mr. Bolan?" a voice asked softly behind him.

He swung around. The young woman was leaning against the wall, just inside the bedroom door. She wore riding breeches and a blazing yellow shirt. Beneath jet-black hair, the even tan of her face glowed against the damask wall. Her lips were full and sensuous, and the breasts swelling from below the open neck of her shirt were lush and ripe.

Bolan smiled. "Should I know you?"

"Holman. Katrina Holman," she replied. There was a Latin huskiness to her voice, but he couldn't place the accent. "I hope you're comfortable. Please consider yourself perfectly free to come and go as you like within the house and grounds—though perhaps I should add that there are reasons why a guest shouldn't stray beyond the boundaries of our . . . hospitality."

"I've seen the dogs, the fence and the hired killers."

"So. You have already been outside? That's good. You will perhaps then—"

"What I want to know is why I'm here," Bolan cut in brusquely.

Katrina Holman was carrying a braided leather riding crop. She tapped it impatiently against the booted curve of one calf. "All in good time, Mr. Bolan," she said. "For the moment, I'm sure you must agree that our confinement is hardly oppressive. As far as motives and reasons go, Mr. Latta will enlighten you in due course."

"Mr. Latta?"

"Your host. He'll be back later. Unfortunately he had to go into the city."

"What city?"

The young woman smiled. "The nearest city. Perhaps Mr. Latta will be able to explain more than I can. But I know he would want me to emphasize that the main reason you're here is because we want to enjoy your company and your conversation."

"With or without electrodes?" Bolan queried.

The girl laughed. "It should be a stimulating evening for all three of us."

"What's your angle? Are you a stimulator too? Or do you just look after the prisoners?"

"A bit of both perhaps. But in the latter role, I have to warn you that you'll find things all over the house that could be used as weapons—cutlery, golf clubs, tire irons, billiard cues, wrenches, even African spears. They've been freely left around, however, simply because Mr. Latta is certain, and I do mean certain, that there would be no point in anyone trying to use them. The guards are everywhere, and they never miss."

"I see," Bolan said. "I'm more interested in knowing where I am and why I'm here."

Katrina Holman merely smiled. "Dinner is at eight-thirty. We usually have a cocktail at eight in the library, and we'd be happy if you would join us. You'll find the door at the end of the entrance hall, below the gallery. If there's anything you need before then, just ring."

She raised the riding crop in a mock salute and left him.

The Executioner's pockets had been emptied, but in the bathroom adjoining his own room he found shaving gear laid out, and a white silk shirt with a selection of ties on his bed. A dark suit that fitted him quite well was hanging in the closet. He shaved, showered and dressed. At ten minutes past eight o'clock, when the clatter of pots, pans and dishes was audible someplace below his window, he went downstairs.

The library was immense: three walls were lined floor-to-ceiling with shelves filled with books, the fourth wall covered by carved paneling that surrounded a hooded chimney over a log fire. The books looked as though they'd all been read.

Katrina was standing at a rosewood table beneath the central chandelier. Glass in hand, the wide, bulky man beside her, who topped Bolan's six feet three inches, looked like a young Orson Welles on an off day. "Mr. Bolan!" he exclaimed, moving forward with a surprisingly catlike tread. "One does so apologize for the, ah, unconventional form of your invitation. But it *is* good to see you perpendicular at last."

"'Praise while you can the vertical man,'" Bolan misquoted with a crooked smile, "'so soon to become the horizontal one'?"

"Now you mustn't feel like that," Latta reproached. "One admits a certain theatricality about the means employed to get you here, about the machinery of ensuring that you stay. But then that's inseparable from the presence of a guest who might wish to leave before one was oneself tired of his company, don't you agree?" The voice was firm and yet mellifluous, a graceful complement to the way the big man moved.

"Look, Latta, if that's your name, the only thing we're likely to agree on is an explanation. Like the reason for my presence here."

"We simply wanted to talk to you, Mr. Bolan. That's all. Really."

Katrina, standing between them, was wearing a low-necked dress in plum-colored velvet. The overhead light sculpted the soft flesh of her shoulders and hollowed with shadow the slopes of her breasts. "What will you have, Mr. Bolan? A dry Martini? A whiskey? Bourbon?"

"Scotch."

She moved across to the wall, dark nylons gleaming, and tugged at an old-fashioned bellpull. A moment later, a saturnine servant appeared in the doorway. Behind him, Bolan saw the shape of one of the gunmen in the shadows beneath the staircase. "Scotch for our guest," the woman said, "and two more whiskey sours for Mr. Latta and me."

While they waited for dinner, both Latta and Katrina kept the conversation general. They talked about New York theater, West Coast jazz, European sports cars, Muslim fundamentalism in the Middle East. Bolan didn't understand what the hell was going on, but it suited him to play a waiting game, and since neither of his "hosts" made a reference to the fact that he was a prisoner, he was content to leave everything at this artificial level until the servant reappeared to announce that dinner was served.

Katrina took his arm and led the way to the dining room. Feeling self-conscious and slightly out of place, like the guy who opens the wrong door and finds himself on stage in the second act of a drawing room comedy, the Executioner moved with her.

The meal was excellent, and both Latta and the woman were well-read, well-informed, even charming. Bolan had to keep reminding himself of his predicament. Even so, he found himself actually involved in a discussion on the alternatives open to a security chief faced with the demands of skyjackers holding a planeload of hostages. It wasn't until the servant circulated with the cheese board that the first loaded question was insinuated.

"In your own work, Mr. Bolan," Latta said casually, "I suppose more than half your assignments concern some villainy or other perpetrated by the Mafia. You don't find that this, uh, specialization blunts your concentration for other missions?"

The question took the warrior by surprise, but his face betrayed no change of expression.

It was an awkward query just the same. It would be stupid, in the circumstances, to pretend he didn't know what the guy was talking about. It was clear, too, that his captor must be familiar with his longtime vendetta against the Mob, and that Bolan was involved in certain "missions." Yet not knowing who or what the big man was, he was unwilling to give a straight answer. He decided to stall.

"Any kind of undercover operative," he said, "whether he's a cop, a spook, an Army intelligence agent or whatever, learns to regard every mission as though it were his first. Each one is a whole new deal. And I don't know where you get your figures, not to mention your intel, but I could hardly confirm your fifty-percent-plus estimate."

Latta was smiling. "Or deny?"

"Or deny," he agreed, nodding.

"Oh, come now, Mr. Bolan! In my business," the other said, as an oil king might say to a movie tycoon, "in my business one is bound to come up against a mass of facts and figures concerning the Mafia. It would be unnatural if one didn't—like being in the car-racing game without having heard of Ferrari."

"And just what is your business, Latta?"

"We're both adults, Mr. Bolan. I see no point in elaborate fencing. It bores me and it achieves nothing. In any case, it must be obvious to you that I operate on the wrong side of the law."

"The thought occurred to me."

"But as to a precise description...What would you say, my dear?"

"I would say you're in the transport business," Katrina said.

Latta was delighted. "Exactly!" he exclaimed. "I'm in the transport business...the transportation of items of value, shall we say, from one locality to another."

"That could cover safecracking, bank robbery, espionage, smuggling, drugs or the white-slave trade," Bolan replied.

"So it could, Mr. Bolan. So it could. But you could say that I dabble in economics as well, you know. Talking of which, do you find that the Mafia keep abreast of the remarkable advance in communication techniques we see today? Would you allow that their telecommunications and computer setup, for instance, compares with that of Stony Man Farm?"

Bolan set his wineglass carefully on the table. "A man of your intelligence can hardly expect a specific answer to that," he said. The guy would know about Brognola's safehouse, sure, because that was where they'd planned and successfully carried out the kidnapping. But how in hell did he know about Stony Man, the secret base in Virginia's Blue Ridge Mountains from which Bolan himself had once masterminded an antiterrorist campaign secretly funded by the American government?

Before he could come up with an answer to that one, Latta had deftly channeled the subject in another direction, and the question of the Executioner's profession wasn't raised again until the following day. They had coffee and brandy, and talked about nuclear fuels for the generation of electricity. Then they went to bed, and in the morning Bolan was left to his own devices while Katrina played nine holes on a miniature golf course laid out in the grounds. Latta didn't appear until noon, but Bolan was never out of sight of one or more of the armed guards.

The day was warm enough for lunch to be served beneath a striped parasol on the terrace. The subject of communications was raised almost at once. Katrina began, "In any operation, the initial advantage is always with the lawbreaker, the attacker's advantage of surprise. But once the law rows in all the software and hardware available, it's supposed to swing the balance the other way. Don't you think, though, that sophisticated computer techniques might in fact delay things, once operatives in the field start reporting?''

"I don't see why," Bolan said.

"Because any plan would have to be constantly amended. Every report would materially alter the global situation, and would have to be taken into account before the next stage of the plan evolved."

"So?"

"So although your computer *decides* quickly, in a fraction of a second, and comes up with an instant answer, the time taken to prepare it for that must surely cancel the advantage of its operating time. After all, top men can decide quickly, too. That's why they're top men. All they have to do is evaluate and deal with a telephone message, a written report, or something equally immediate."

"Probably."

"What I mean is I'm not at all sure they wouldn't be better off using those old-fashioned human error methods—at least as far as the time element is concerned."

"Undercover strategy isn't as simple as that," Bolan said, wondering where this surprisingly naive line of reasoning was to lead. "Tactics, either." He decided to hold out a carrot. "You're forgetting the quality of the relative plans, human versus electronic," he said. "We live in a technical age. It's not always a case of an operative making a simple phone call, is it?"

She took a bite of the carrot at once. "Ah, you mean the more sophisticated means of communication—microdot messages, scrambled radio transmissions, sub-visual photography, coded frequencies that actuate telex machines. That kind of thing?''

''That's right.''

''But surely those take just as much time to organize as the programming of a computer? Still, I guess high-powered antisocial groups like the Mafia or the 'Holy War' terrorists in the Middle East would have to keep abreast of the latest developments to stay in business, wouldn't they?''

''Would they?''

Latta smiled and joined the conversation for the first time. ''Of course they would—and do. You know that as well as I do, Mr. Bolan. What *do* they use? What do you use yourself, when you want to get in touch with your headquarters?''

''I don't have any headquarters,'' Bolan replied. ''I work alone. If I want to make contact with anyone, I send a postcard.''

Katrina Holman laughed. ''You probably do at that. Would you like another cup of coffee?''

Pacing alone across the lawns later in the afternoon, the warrior analyzed the various conversations as minutely as he could.

It was puzzling enough to have been grabbed between missions and taken to some country retreat apparently far from Washington, doubly puzzling to find himself wined and dined and indulged in intellectual conversation. But what fazed him most of all was the reaction of his captors—or the lack of it—to his evasion of the loaded questions carefully introduced into all this good living.

They said they wanted to talk to him . . . and that was all. So far this seemed to be true. And the subject, disguise it as they would, was clearly communications—either Brognola's or the Mob's. Yet each time Bolan blocked or ignored the question, they dropped the subject with perfect good humor and never returned to it. Somehow, it didn't add up: it seemed a crazy approach for people who had gone to such trouble to get him there!

As far as he could see, there was only one explanation for the facts he had. And if he was right, then he was in big trouble.

First, though, he had to double-check. He would float out a decoy during dinner and see if it was taken.

The opportunity came halfway through the meal. Latta had adroitly led the conversation from the population explosion, through the approaching world food shortage and modern dietetics, to famine and natural catastrophe in general. And from there it was a short stop to measures designed to combat such dramas.

Which of course involved communications.

"In such universal cases," Bolan said, "where there's no question of lawbreaking of people on the run, what's wrong with the radio or a satellite link?"

"Oh, but my dear fellow, just think!" Latta protested. "What about an outbreak of bubonic plague, lethal fallout, the news that a country's water supply had been contaminated, anything that could cause panic? Surely news of that kind must be transmitted in a way that hides its meaning from the casual eye? When a leak could lead to riots?"

"As you were saying yesterday, there are codes, microfilms—"

"Yes, yes. But suppose, for example, you discovered an unknown virus was threatening the rice crop in India, and a neighboring country was aiming to exploit that. You'd want to transmit all the details to the FAO, maybe the Security Council. You'd have to furnish the data and let them decide for themselves if your theory was correct. And yet nobody must see the material you send in case you are wrong—or in case it provides panic in the population.''

''Yeah, well, the first thing would be—''

''You'd have to send graphs, tables, maybe photos of the affected plants, all kinds of stuff to support your written report. How would you do it?''

''I see what you mean,'' Katrina said, as though the dialogue hadn't been rehearsed. ''Pictures by radio and wire can be intercepted, microfilms can be developed, and documents can be photocopied. If there were other people equally interested in seeing your report, and you must at all costs prevent them, what would you do?'' She looked at the Executioner.

''Yes,'' Latta echoed, ''what would you do, Mr. Bolan? Use one of the communications satellites, make a hologram, scramble them with lasers? Do give us a professional view.''

It was the perfect opportunity for Bolan to push out his decoy. ''If there were other people after the intel, people who knew I had it,'' he said, ''I'd be much more worried about them finding out the details from me than from any messages I sent. Hell, the advances in the field of stupefiants, subliminal narcotics and so-called truth drugs, even in the past five years, have been literally mind-blowing.''

Latta killed the subject stone dead. Interrupting Bolan with a brusque apology, he summoned the servant and made a vicious complaint about a strawberry shortcake that was entirely blameless. And then, as soon as the man removed it and went to fetch something else, he dived straight into an analysis of ''the servant problem'' before Bolan could pick up the threads of his argument. But the warrior didn't give a damn: the change of subject had told him exactly what he wanted to know. By inference at least, his deductions were confirmed.

He knew now why he'd been kidnapped between missions—and why his captors didn't give a good goddamn whether he answered their questions or not.

UNDERCOVER INTELLIGENCE OPERATIVES, penetration agents, various kinds of spooks in the field and their shadow executives, when they possess highly sensitive information, will probably undergo a type of subliminal conditioning designed to resist brainwashing.

The treatment, which involves deep hypnosis and is still highly classified, ensures that the operative will come across with certain prepared replies under the influence of truth drugs, hostile hypnosis or torture. It is given immediately after the operative has been briefed.

In principle it implants into the subconscious a succession of conditioned reflexes to any questions concerning the mission when the conscious mind is withdrawn. Like all good lies, it steers as near the truth as possible, for it can never be calculated how much a hostile interrogator already knows, and if he finds the subject confirms facts already in his possession, he will be all the readier to believe the fantasy that follows.

The conditioning provides a valid reason for all an agent's actions that, despite the fact that it *fits* the facts, is very far from the true one.

It's almost impossible to successfully pump an agent treated in this way: even if, in the extremities of torture, the guy *wants* to talk, the conditioning will impose on him the false rather than the true line.

Between missions, of course, agents aren't subjected to the treatment.

And Mack Bolan was between missions....

In fact, apart from one or two extra-delicate missions for the government that had taken him behind the iron curtain, Bolan had never as a loner been conditioned in this way.

Evidently his kidnappers were unaware of this. Still, there was a mass of secret, high-tech and organizational intel locked in his mind. And he was vulnerable to any ultramodern system of drugs—whether secretly administered in his food and drink or pumped into him openly and forcibly—that his captors chose to use.

Now he realized why it didn't matter if he answered their questions or not. They were simply to put certain subjects, communications, for instance, and the Mafia, in the forefront of his mind. The real questions would come later when his subconscious mind, unconditioned to resist, would be at the mercy of whatever treatment they had in store for him.

Whoever they were—and it was patently clear, despite their apparently outside interest, they were themselves connected with the Mafia—it was obvious that they badly needed some particular information they figured he had to have.

And they couldn't afford to allow the subject of drugs to come up in the conversation in case he tumbled to the connection and it tipped him off.

Now that he *had* tumbled, he had just one priority.

Get the hell out. Fast.

Speculation on what it was they wanted to pry out of him could wait. Right now he had to find a way of getting past the guards, the dogs and the electric fence.

5

He would have to escape.

The moon would be full, and the guards would certainly be at their most alert after dark. But Bolan was a past master in the use of ground cover, and the shadows would give him a good chance of reaching the boundary fence unseen.

More importantly, the time element was vital. He'd already been allowed forty-eight hours of good living to soften him up for the drug-aided interrogation they must have planned. Yet their need for whatever intel Bolan possessed had to be urgent: the crack organization of the kidnapping proved that. Phase two had to be imminent.

Yeah, maybe that crack about drugs had been ill-advised after all.

There were very few preparations he could make. He'd decided to leave the house via the roof. Doors and windows would be monitored by alarms that would sound whichever way the threshold was crossed. And he'd observed a trapdoor above the stairwell. To cross the electrified fence he'd need a rope, and he hoped to find one in the garages. Finally there were the dogs...and he figured he could deal with these, literally, out of his own head.

A crown covering one of his molars unscrewed to reveal a tiny cavity. On ultrasensitive operations he normally hid two tiny pellets of a quick-acting knockout drug inside.

He had managed to slip two slices of duck into his pocket during the diversionary dispute over the strawberry shortcake. Bolan took the napkin containing the meat from a bureau drawer, removed the pellets from the hollow tooth and then ground them to a fine powder with the handle of his razor. He smeared the white dust over the meat.

The warrior dressed himself in the clothes he'd been wearing when he was kidnapped and settled down to wait.

Latta and Katrina slept at opposite ends of the long upper hallway. The servant had a small suite of rooms off the kitchen, and the guards, who worked in relays, were billeted in the servants' wing.

It was after midnight before the sounds of activity ceased and the household settled down to sleep, but Bolan waited another full hour before he stirred.

At two-fifteen, water gushed from a tap for thirty seconds or so somewhere downstairs. Thirty minutes later, a dog barked and then was silent. Bolan eased open his door as three o'clock struck from the clock tower above the stables. When he heard the single chime that signaled the half hour, he began to make his way silently along the hallway toward the stairs.

The sky was clear, and the foyer below was barred with pale swathes of moonlight falling in through deep windows over the front door.

The trap was clearly visible in the gloom. But first Bolan had to make a trip downstairs. Placing his weight with infinite care on the outside of each tread, he stole down to the ground floor and trod softly through the drawing room and on into the gunroom. He had memorized the positions of the furniture, but the draperies were still drawn and the journey was difficult. Once he came within an inch of stumbling over a coffee table laden with cups and saucers that must have been moved after he'd gone to bed. But at last he was standing in pitch darkness by the billiard table in the gunroom, listening to the silence.

He picked up the long-handled cue rest, with its X-shaped brass end, and started back the way he'd come.

Bolan had just left the coffee-and-cigar-smelling closeness of the drawing room when he froze, then backed into the shadows below the stairs. Through the French windows leading to the terrace, he saw the shadow of a man fall across the flagstones as one of the guards crossed the corner of the moonlit lawn. The outline of his submachine gun was clearly visible.

When it became clear that the guy wasn't returning immediately, Bolan regained the upper hallway. He picked up his shoes and slung them around his neck by the laces. Outside Latta's door he could hear a steady snoring. Katrina's was ajar, and he paused several minutes before he was satisfied that the faint sounds of breathing were deep and regular enough to mean that she slept. At last he was ready. It was time to act.

Climbing onto the carved wood newel post at the top of the stairs, the Executioner poised himself carefully and extended the cue rest, lodging the brass head against the trapdoor. He extended his arms and pushed.

The trap was counterbalanced to remain open once it was pushed upward, rather than fall backward with a bang onto the floor of the loft. As long as it was working the way it should.

He shoved a little harder. With the smallest of creaks, the door freed itself from the frame and swung back into the darkness.

Straining, Bolan pushed harder with the cue rest. The opening yawned wider, the door rose higher and higher. When it was almost completely vertical, presenting the minimum face to his thrust, the metal X slipped on the painted wood with a slight scraping noise.

The warrior froze, senses on full alert. Latta gave an extra loud snore and turned over in his sleep...and a moment later the door fell away from the cue rest to rest in the open position against the pressure of its hydraulic stop.

Bolan released his breath in a sigh of relief. He lowered the cue rest gingerly to the floor and leaned it against the wall. Then he prepared to jump.

Perched on the post with one foot on either side of the wooden ball decorating it, he was in a poor position for an upward swing. But it was the only way to go.

The trap was a couple feet above the tips of his fingers as he balanced there with outstretched arms. Tensing the muscles of his toes, he flexed his knees and leaped.

The sole of one foot slipped slightly on the polished wood as he took off, so that only the fingers of his left hand hit the frame of the trapdoor, clenched, and frenziedly held on. For a timeless moment he hung over the stairwell, his whole weight swinging on those fingers.

It he couldn't hold on, he'd drop to the entrance hall below. And such a fall—even if it didn't break his back— would bring the entire household on him before he could blink an eye.

Bolan scrabbled for a hold with his right hand, found it and began the muscle-racking task of hoisting his body up and through the gap.

By the time he was out of the moonlit dusk of the landing and free to flop down in the musty darkness of the loft, sweat was trickling between his shoulder blades. For two minutes he lay there listening, then he rose cautiously to his knees and lowered the trapdoor into place again.

Twenty minutes later, after what seemed an eternity of groping through the blackness, always fearing he would step on a joist that creaked, he was letting himself out through a tiny attic dormer onto a slope of shingled roof.

The moon was riding high between banks of cloud that had blown up from the south, its milky light streaming down to throw stables, wall, garage and trees into sharp relief, like the cardboard cutouts of a toy farm. Between them, the ground was dense with shadows.

And somewhere in those shadows, probably, would be at least one of Latta's hardguys with an Ingram. Bolan shrugged. The hell with it. Guards or no guards, he had to move fast.

If drugs had been planted in the food he'd eaten, they'd have affected him by now, and he'd been careful to select portions from dishes that Latta and Katrina shared. What was more likely—if his hunch that he'd be questioned tonight was correct—was that they intended to surprise him while he slept, perhaps around four o'clock when resistance was supposedly at its lowest ebb. Which could mean any time after the next half hour. Latta could have an alarm set to awaken him at four. He could be awake already. And in either case the Executioner had to be clear of the house before someone discovered his absence and raised an alarm.

Creeping to the shadowed side of the roof, he found a vent pipe, tested it and lowered himself over the eaves trough.

The descent was surprisingly easy. The pipe was sturdy, and firmly anchored to the wall. Taking advantage of the excellent grip it offered, Bolan climbed down and rounded the corner of the terrace on stockinged feet.

Beyond a shallow flight of steps bordered by classical urns, a stretch of moonlit lawn separated him from the shadowed side of the garage.

The warrior had no time for a recon. The walking silhouette he'd seen from the hallway had been moving in the direction he was traveling now. He had to gamble that the guy's patrol was hourly or half-hourly, in which case he should still have a couple minutes before the gunner was due again. He'd have to risk it.

Bolan sprang down the steps and padded across the lawn.

After the darkness of the house the brightness of the moon was like a slap in the face. He felt as vulnerable as a high-wire artist until he gained the shadows lying along one side of the old brick building.

Nobody called out an alarm. He melted around the corner and tried the garage doors.

As he had hoped, they weren't locked. Set into the wide outer doors was a smaller pass door that swung open noiselessly as he turned the handle. He slipped through and drew it shut behind him.

He could make out the dim shapes of four vehicles in the reflected light filtering through the windows: a station wagon, a Cadillac stretch limo and two small foreign cars, one a sedan and the other a convertible. Although the Caddy's vast trunk yawned obediently open as soon as he touched the button, he drew a blank when he felt around for the rope he needed. The carpeted space was completely empty. With the station wagon, however, he had better luck. Lifting the rear door, he found exactly what he was looking for in the space behind the third row of seats: a coil of towing rope about twelve feet long, with a small iron grappling hook spliced onto one end.

Easing the rope from beneath the roll of tools, Bolan wound it around his waist beneath his jacket. Then he untied the shoes from around his neck and put them on. He was ready to go.

For a moment he toyed with the idea of trying to find out from the license plates of the cars what state he was in. But there wasn't enough light to read them, and the letters and figures were unfamiliar to his touch. He was also aware that he was running out of time: the stable clock had chimed four times several minutes ago.

He stole back to the garage door, eased it open . . . and remained rigid, his hand on the latch.

Four yards away, a man stood with his back to the garage, looking up at the house. Holding his breath, Bolan followed the direction of his gaze. All along the mellow, ivy-covered facade and the slope of shingles above, the dark windows shone with the reflected light of the moon.

All except one.

Of the four attic dormers piercing the roof, one gaped open. In the silver light that streamed down from the sky and bathed every imperfection in the brickwork, the window Bolan had inadvertently left open stood out significantly.

The guard stood there several seconds longer. And then, shifting the Ingram so that his right hand clutched the pistol grip, he turned slowly to scrutinize the moonlit gardens.

Luckily for the Executioner, the moon had moved far enough since he'd entered the garage for the shadow of the gable to fall across the doors. He would have to rely on the contrast of light and shade to hide the fact that the door was half open, since he didn't have a chance to close it now.

The guard's eyes swept past the garage and on toward the corner of the house. Then, apparently coming to a decision, the man strode away toward the front entrance. As he walked, he unclipped a walkie-talkie from his belt and spoke quietly into it.

As soon as the gunner was out of sight, Bolan was through the doorway and sprinting in the other direction. The guard could be making a duty call-in, but it was more likely that he was reporting the open window—either to the head of security or to Latta himself. In which case the Executioner's absence would be discovered in a matter of seconds.

Treading silently on rubber soles, the warrior hurried past the stables and skirted the wall enclosing the garden. A sweep of graveled driveway and a strip of lawn separated him from the long expanse of the parkland. He waited, cursing the haste that had caused him to leave that window open, until the moon sailed behind a cloud bank. Then he dashed across.

The fine stones crunched loudly beneath his feet, but he was past caring now whether people heard him or not—reaching the fence was the only thing that mattered. He raced toward the trees near the boundary of the estate.

Bolan had decided to make his attempt where the electric wires were nearest the house, reasoning that the highest concentration of guards would probably be posted on the other side, where the fence was the farthest away.

It was a lucky choice, now that every second turned out to be vital. He had two hundred yards to go, and al-

ready, glancing over his shoulder, he saw that lights had
come on behind the main doors of the house.

When he was thirty yards from the fence, the warrior
dropped to the ground and pressed his face to the damp
grass. He'd seen the dim figure of a guard running across
an open area on the far side of the shrubbery. The man
had obviously been called up to the house.

Seconds later the warrior was standing beneath a tall
cedar tree just inside the chain-link fence. He took the
strips of the doctored meat from his pocket and un-
coiled the rope from around his waist. Then, playing out
about six feet of the end with the hook attached, he
looped the rest over his wrist and began whirling the free
end around his head.

As Bolan stared up at the dark mass of the tree, trying
to choose a suitable branch to aim for, he heard a slight
noise on his flank.

One of the guards stood at the edge of the shrubbery
with his Ingram raised to fire.

Bolan's fighter reflexes saved his life. Lightning-fast,
he increased the length of the rope and dropped his wrist.
The heavy iron hook altered its trajectory, whistling
through the air in a slight arc to smash into the side of the
gunman's head.

The guard stiffened, dropped his weapon and crashed
back among the bushes.

Bolan stole a glance over his shoulder. Windows blazed
with light all along the upper floor of the house. At any
moment his empty room would be discovered.

He retrieved the Ingram and then whirled the rope
above his head, casting upward for a tangle of boughs
that was visible about sixteen feet from the ground. On
the third attempt, the hook caught firmly enough for the
rope to take his weight. He lobbed the pieces of drugged

meat over the fence into the space between the wire and the outer wall.

He didn't see the dogs, but they were on the stuff in an instant, a blur of black-and-tan bodies snarling and snuffling in the dark as they fought over the meat.

Bolan was halfway up the rope, swinging like a pendulum, before the Dobermans had swallowed the food. As they staggered and sank to the ground, he rocketed the rope, Tarzanlike, to its zenith and let go as he rose toward the electrified fence.

He felt a rush of air against his face, followed by a jarring impact that shook every bone in his body. He went into a shoulder roll as he landed and came up in a combat crouch . . . but for the moment he was safe. He'd fallen in the center of the cleared strip between the fence and the wall.

As he rose to his full height, the moon swam out from behind the cloud bank, flooding the area with light. At the same time he heard a clamor of voices burst from the house. They had realized that the bird had flown.

Time for a swift recon.

Fifty yards to his left, where the wire fence crossed the main driveway by means of a steel grid, was a gate house. The outer gates were housed in an arch piercing the building, so there was no hope of escape that way. As he watched, floodlight blazed into life above the arch. Others glowed and then dazzled at intervals around the perimeter.

Bolan turned to the right . . . and tensed.

A third Doberman stared at him over the prostrate bodies of its kennel mates. Bolan took one look at the murderous glare of its eyes and exploded into action.

He tossed the Ingram over the wall, wrenched off his jacket and rushed toward the dog uttering a growl that he hoped would sound like a snarl of rage. For an instant the animal, taken by surprise, backed off with its hackles raised. And in that moment the warrior swerved aside and leaped for the wall.

He flung up the jacket, which caught miraculously on a shard of broken glass that glittered along the top of the brickwork, grabbed the material and swung his feet clear as the guard dog snapped at his heels.

Seconds later he had hauled himself up and dropped soundlessly to a stretch of grass on the far side. Bolan saw a white road that traversed a dream landscape of moon-lit woods and fields. He picked up the Ingram and started to run as the Doberman on the other side of the wall began to bark furiously.

The road was featureless. No trees or bushes separated the soft shoulder from farmland on which some crop was only just showing above the furrowed earth. The nearest stand of trees was a quarter of a mile away.

An engine revved loudly and gravel scattered as a car sped down the estate's driveway and out the main gate. Powerful headlights silhouetted Bolan's running figure. The vehicle would be on him in seconds.

The Executioner turned aside and jumped into a low drainage ditch at the side of the road. Panting, he lay prone and pulled out the Ingram's telescopic metal stock. He aimed at the oncoming vehicle.

The small convertible was traveling fast with the top down. As far as Bolan could see, the vehicle contained three men. He guessed they weren't wise to the fact that he'd taken a weapon from one of their confederates because one gunner was standing up beside the driver, resting his submachine gun on top of the windshield, and the third man sat on the top of the trunk with his feet on the rear seat.

An instant before they opened fire, Bolan heard a second car scream out of the gates and take off down the road in the other direction.

Flame spit from the muzzle of the gun propped on the windshield; at the same time Bolan squeezed his trigger. The silenced Ingram shuddered in his grasp as a burst of .45-caliber ACP rounds snorted out the grooved suppressor to shatter the convertible's headlights.

A volley of slugs peppered the earth around the warrior. He let loose with another burst, watching the windshield erupt in a silver fountain and the guy above it spin backward into the road with outflung arms.

The driver braked, wrenching the car around with shrieking tires, and the rear gunner ducked out of sight, flaming a long burst at the ditch. But the Executioner had hosed a deathstream at the guy behind the wheel, blowing him away.

The car crashed into the ditch and flipped over onto its side, stalling the engine. Alloy spokes glinted in the wan light as a rear wheel turned slowly to a halt beneath the moon.

The rear gunner had been thrown clear and lay sprawled in the road, half hidden by the capsized convertible. His Ingram was ten feet away.

Crawling swiftly on hands and knees he made a grab for it, but Bolan leaned sideways to get a wider angle on the target and hammered out a long burst, catching the guy before he reached his goal.

The stream of flesh-shredders didn't kill the gunner, but the impact knocked him over backward, screaming. He rolled into the ditch on the other side of the road and disappeared.

The Executioner squeezed the Ingram's trigger again, hoping to keep the man's head down, and heard nothing but a hollow click. He was out of ammunition.

There would be ammo left in the gunners' weapon, but one was underneath the car and the other thirty yards away in the middle of the road. Should he take a chance and race back to retrieve it?

No way. Drawn by the sound of protesting tires and the yell of the wounded gunner in the ditch, reinforcements on foot were crowding out of the gateway of the estate and running in his direction. There was a chance, too, that the hardguy he hit would possess a handgun.

Bolan got to his feet and took off toward the woods.

He had guessed right. Ten paces from his hiding place, he heard the deep-throated reports of a heavy-caliber revolver. A slug whined off a stone in the road, followed by another that whistled dangerously close to Bolan's ear. He tossed away the useless Ingram and poured on as much speed as his muscles could supply, weaving from side to side as he powered effortlessly away from the immobilized shooter.

Four more shots rang out, and then only the more distant sounds of pursuit, including the exhaust blare of two more vehicles being gunned to the maximum.

Beyond the woods the road dipped and forked left, right across a more undulating landscape. There were no direction signs where the road branched.

Bolan glanced hastily each way. He had hoped at first—even when they discovered he was missing—that his captors wouldn't know whether he'd escaped hours ago or only recently. The dogs and the roadside battle had killed that one. They knew he couldn't have gotten far; they didn't need to waste time and manpower searching beyond the immediate vicinity of the estate.

Put it another way: he had to find a place to hide. Fast.

He took the left-hand fork. A mile away, on top of a rise, the long, low outbuildings of a farm bulked against the moonlit sky. It was the obvious place for his pursuers to look—so he'd go to ground before he made it that far.

Fifty yards ahead, a gate led into a large field surrounded with hedgerows, and between the gate and the road was a cattle grid—an iron grille placed over a depression in the ground to deter livestock from straying off their owner's property.

With great effort Bolan pried up the heavy grid, dropped into the space below it and lowered it cautiously back into place.

For what seemed like many hours, with the sweat drying cold on his body, he lay there with his face pressed close to the musty earth. Several cars swept past two or three times, and once a spotlight moved slowly along the hedgerow as a vehicle ground past in low gear. Bars of illumination fingered the dark in the Executioner's self-chosen prison, fanning out over a slope of mud to reveal a tuft of blanched leaves, a spider scurrying, the gluey end of a worm. Sometime later he heard the sounds of footsteps hurrying by. Finally all was quiet.

Bolan placed his shoulders beneath the grille and pushed it up. He stood, stretched and surveyed the terrain. The moon had sunk below the horizon, and the meadows lay spread out beneath the dark sky as far as he could see. But however far the vehicular pursuit had ranged, he was sure Latta would've left sentries in the immediate vicinity of the house. To keep to the road would be suicidal: he knew he had to travel across country until it was safe enough to hitch a ride to the nearest town.

He swung over the gate and hurried away from the road along the boundary of the field. In the distance he heard a single chime struck from the clock above Latta's stables.

Five-thirty.

Half a mile farther he reached a line of trees stretching away to the east, where a faint lightening of the sky told him dawn wasn't far off. Ten minutes later he was standing on top of a bank above a narrow country lane.

He looked left and right along the ghostly strip of road, but could see no signs of his pursuers. He plunged down the bank and set off at a trot in the direction that seemed farthest from the Latta property, still heading east.

Soon he saw lights flick on in a cottage on the far side of a field. A rooster crowed and a dog barked in the distance. Far away across the dark countryside a low, wide structure was silhouetted against the paling sky. It looked like an overpass carrying a state highway above the flatland; and indeed when Bolan stopped he could hear the hum of traffic and make out the moving blurs of cars and trucks above the concrete supports.

A little later, the lane curved around a stand of willows and he came to a T-shaped intersection. It was quite light by now, and against the far hedge—at last—he could make out a road sign.

Bolan halted. For a moment he stared at the sign. The directions were in an unfamiliar white lettering on an enameled blue background. His eyes widened, and his mouth dropped open in disbelief.

The right-hand board said Houdemelle 15 km. The one on the left announced Couette 9 km. And above this was a separate, rectangular sign, a green one on which white characters spelled out the legend:

Autoroute E.9: Luxembourg-Liège—2000 m

Bolan shook his head, amazed. Small wonder he'd found "foreign" automobiles in Latta's garage, with unfamiliar license plates. No surprise that he couldn't place the landscape.

Vermont or Wisconsin, hell! Far from spiriting him to a distant state in the Union, the kidnappers had flown him clear across the Atlantic and he was now in the southeast corner of Belgium.

6

It was three minutes to ten, and the sun was high in a cloudless sky before conditions were right for the Executioner to act.

He had walked a couple of miles along the foot of the embankment that carried the expressway when he saw the white "P" on a blue rectangle that signaled a rest area one thousand meters ahead. Then, after he'd made it up the bank to the parking lot to wait for a ride, everything went wrong.

Nobody pulled off the road for two hours. The early-morning drivers were commuters with no time to spare; the truckers had too recently stopped for coffee, or were too eager to make the city before the rush hour traffic fouled up the streets.

After that, a succession of cars, panel trucks and semis drew up, waited and pulled away again. But they stopped several at a time, or the cars had passengers, or the driver didn't get out. It did not work out the way Bolan wanted it.

He lay concealed in the long grass, sweating. His jacket had been left behind on top of the wall that surrounded Latta's property, and at first, in the chill air of dawn, he had missed it. Now with the heat of the midmorning sun beating on his back, he wished he'd left his shirt as well. Ears numbed by the continuous roar of traffic on the expressway, he squinted his eyes against the glare and gazed over the twin ribbons of concrete at a landscape of small fields and trees misted with spring green.

He'd never heard of Couette or Houdemelle, but he knew that Luxembourg city and Liège were about eighty miles apart. If he was between them he had to be near the forests of the Ardennes. And when alone in a foreign country, with no money, no ID, no weapons and no clothes except those he was wearing, what he needed was a city.

A city from which he could somehow make a panic call home.

Which was nearer, Luxembourg or Liège?

Did it matter? The rest area was on the northbound lane of the expressway; he'd have to go that way when he was able to commandeer a vehicle, which was what he had to do next.

But it wasn't going to be easy. There was nothing in the pockets of his pants, so it would have to be a car with the key in the ignition; it would have to be a car with a driver and no passengers; the driver would have to get out of the vehicle after it stopped and lastly, Bolan would have to wait until a vehicle that met all those conditions drew up when the lot was empty.

An extra hazard: the car had to be powerful enough to make the city exit before the dispossessed driver could reach a phone and give the alarm.

Bolan thought he'd finally gotten lucky when a Mercedes 190 carrying only the driver pulled in just after a whole string of trucks had left. But the young guy at the wheel never left the sedan. He ate a boxed lunch behind the wheel, smoked a leisurely cigarette without leaving his seat and then drove off.

Another time, a middle-aged woman left a Volvo with the engine running while she scrambled around a stand of trees on the other side of the lot picking wildflowers. The warrior had actually been on his feet when two Dutch oil tankers lumbered up and parked just beyond the car.

But at last it happened. The lot was empty, and a fat man driving a big Datsun arrived and stopped with a squeal of brakes. He got out, looked around, then plunged into the bushes fifty yards away from Bolan, unzipping his pants on the run. And the Executioner, rising like a phoenix from his grassy bed, sprinted across the pavement, jerked open the door and slid into the driver's seat.

He twisted the ignition key, put the vehicle into first and swung the wheel hard over to head back toward the expressway.

The warrior had a momentary impression in the rearview mirror of a shouting figure waving his arms, and then he was away, stomping the pedal flat against the floor as the Datsun snarled down the concrete strip toward Liège.

If the enraged owner relied on the roadside phones the Executioner would probably be okay. But if a highway patrolman happened to pass the lot, things might get tough. Flashing past the midmorning traffic on the heat-shimmered pavement, Bolan kept one eye warily on the mirror, on the lookout for a black-and-white sedan with a flashing blue light on the roof, a pair of dark-uniformed motorcycle cops, or the sound of a siren.

It was, in fact, through the windshield that he received a shock. Slantwise across the hard shoulder, he saw the huge sign that said Péage 5000 m.

Of course! Many of the European expressways were toll roads. There was a toll booth ahead, and he didn't have a cent on him....

He flipped open the glove compartment and found a spark plug, a soiled handkerchief, a pile of crumpled candy bar wrappers...but not the handful of forgotten coins he'd hoped for.

Bolan glanced at the instruments. The Datsun was hitting 100 mph. He had less than two minutes to come up with an answer to this immediate problem.

Another sign flashed past and dwindled in the rear-view mirror: Péage 3000 m.

Bolan dived a hand into the deep pocket on his door. Zero. In the pocket on the passenger side? He reached across. Nothing but maps.

Péage 1000 m. Half a mile ahead he could see modernistic flat roofs, the curving stalks of electric standards, the colored stop and go lights of the toll booth. He lifted the leather holder of the car's parking permit from the padded shelf above the dashboard. It was stamped in gold and bore the number of a garage in Brussels.

And beneath it was a pink card marked off in squares—some with holes punched in them—that looked as if it could be a weekly or monthly pass for the expressway.

Braking, the warrior sighed with relief. He'd noticed that the Datsun had Luxembourg license plates; clearly the owner was a regular traveler between the two cities. Bolan shifted to fourth, to third, to second and rolled down his window to hold out the card as the car slid to a halt opposite the uniformed attendant in the toll booth.

The man took the card, swung around in the glass-fronted booth, struck a punch with the flat of his hand and returned the card without a glance at Bolan. He gestured the vehicle forward and pressed a switch to change the light in front of it from red to green.

The Executioner was past the hazard, but he reckoned it was time to split fast: a guy in one of the other booths had been holding a phone to his ear and gesticulating excitedly. It was possible that the call could have already gone out for a stolen Datsun.

The woods and fields gave way to the urban clutter that signaled the outskirts of a city. As the car was sucked into the vortex of traffic swirling toward the center, Bolan saw thin chimneys that belched flame at the sunny sky, vacant lots pockmarked with tin-roof shanties, junkyards piled high with car wrecks. Across the smoky horizon, the city was battlemented with the rectangular slabs of high-rise apartment blocks.

The stream of traffic moved too fast—and the road system was too complex—for Bolan to pick a route. For a while he went with the main flow. Then he found himself in the wrong lane at a big police-controlled junction. And while most of the vehicles swung away unexpectedly to the left, he was obliged to go straight ahead into a maze of narrow streets that led to a riverside warehouse area. To have attempted to cut across the line would have invited attention from the police, which was the last thing he needed. What the hell. He drove on.

Threading the Datsun between the barrows and stalls of a street market bright with fruit and vegetables, he searched for some sign that would lead him back to a main street or toward the city center. But all the streets seemed to be one-way—the wrong way. Like it or not, he was penetrating deeper and deeper into the dock area.

Between the gaunt facades of the warehouses he saw cranes, the blue of the river, the spires of a cathedral on the far side. But there was no sign of a bridge.

Eventually the warrior found himself in a street so choked with pedestrians and off-loading trucks that he had to stop. There were no sidewalks: smooth-worn cobbles joined one row of gray buildings to the other. The car was attracting attention, yet Bolan couldn't leave it in the middle of the street. With no curbs, there was no logical place to park, and the few side streets he'd noticed were already jammed with vehicles that blocked every available space.

At last, in desperation, he edged the sedan forward and turned into a courtyard beyond which was an official-looking building with a wide flight of steps and a flag hanging over the entrance. He stopped the car and climbed out.

"Hey! You!" a voice called out. "What the hell do you think you're doing?"

Bolan swung around. A booted cop in breeches and a leather jacket had been hitching a motorcycle on its stand. Now he was staring angrily at the warrior.

Too late Bolan saw that a blue panel truck with an amber roof light was parked at the end of a line of police cars behind him. He'd driven into the front yard of a police station or a town hall.

The cop was striding toward him, scowling. Bolan decided to avoid the confrontation.

He ran back into the street, darted across and sped along behind a row of market stalls. Footsteps clattered on the cobbles behind him, voices were raised in protest, in question.

The street was blocked fifty yards farther when three men rolled barrels of beer down a ramp from the open door of a trailer. Bolan crossed the street and dashed into an arched cloister.

At the far end of the cloister he found himself in a paved lobby full of elderly men in cassocks. Glass doors opened on steps that led up to a street bright with sunlight.

Bolan ran past the clerics, burst out the doors and took the steps three at a time. A moment later he was hurrying through a press of students thronging a sidewalk café. Two more turns brought him to a wide main street leading uphill from a bridge over the River Meuse.

A long convoy of dun-colored army trucks and half-tracks loaded with soldiers in combat fatigues was lumbering up the grade. Waiting to cross the road, the warrior glanced over his shoulders. He seemed to have shaken off the pursuit.

So what were the options?

He could check the phone book, see if there was an American consul in Liège. He could make it to the embassy in Brussels. But even if they believed his story—and they might not without one hell of an inquest—he was unwilling to involve the country in a personal dilemma that revolved entirely around his status as an unofficial loner who wasn't even on a mission. And although there was a new, unstated, "arms-length" alliance between Bolan and officialdom, there were still plenty of people in the administration who would be happy to see the Executioner in tough shit, who would go out of their way to make sure Bolan stayed down . . . and out. Permanently.

He'd have to get hold of Hal Brognola.

Easier said than done.

The answer came to him as he stepped into the road to pass behind the last truck in the convoy. He remembered speeding past a similar line of army vehicles on the expressway, and he'd been automatically checking out the components of the convoy as he waited: ten three-tonners, a dozen half-tracks, a command truck, two high, square ambulances with huge red crosses painted on their steel sides.

Bolan's idea was a long shot, all right. But if it came off it could give him a shortcut to Brognola. There were no soldiers in the last truck. He swung himself up over the tailgate and dropped into the dark space under the canvas canopy. Forty minutes later he lifted the flap and peered out.

The convoy had halted in a compound of a military encampment, and judging from the commands he heard, the crews had been marched off to the mess hall for chow.

Bolan donned the camouflage fatigues he'd found among the stores in the truck and dropped to the ground.

From what he'd been able to see as the vehicles lurched out of the city, the convoy had stopped about twenty miles southeast of Liège, somewhere near the town of St. Vith and the West German frontier. The camp was surrounded by the wooded hills of the Ardennes.

He lifted a steel helmet covered in netting from the driver's cab and walked nonchalantly toward the head of the convoy.

The command truck was outwardly like the ambulances, but a complex of radio antennas sprouted from its squat roof. And in the boxlike cab, he knew, would be a sophisticated and extremely powerful shortwave transmitter.

Affecting a casual air, Bolan climbed into the cab. He stared out through the windshield at a detail busily erecting a khaki tent beside a row of huts two hundred yards away. Nobody was looking in his direction.

Taking a deep calming breath, Bolan pressed the starter button. The warm engine growled to life, then, for the second time that day, he steered a stolen vehicle out of a parking lot toward the road.

7

"What the *hell*'s going on?" Hal Brognola raged. "A man is grabbed on my own doorstep, witnesses are eliminated, we hear Zulowski's been murdered at the post office in Luxembourg and the pictures he sent are meaningless!" He breathed deeply. "And now State's after my butt because some half-assed American tourist in Belgium stole an army command car and used the radio to send a birthday message to his uncle!"

"If you'd just take a look, sir, at the reports..." Frank O'Reilly gestured toward the folders on Brognola's desk.

"The hell with the reports!" the Fed yelled. "What do I have to do to get people into action around here? And as for this tourist—"

"No tourist," O'Reilly said gently. "Bolan."

"In *Belgium*?"

"That's right, Mr. Brognola."

"How do you know? Why wasn't I told?" Brognola was red in the face.

"You were at a conference in the Oval Office and you weren't able to be disturbed. And we know," the security chief said soothingly, "because the 'birthday message' was a coded request for help." He leaned over the Fed's shoulder and flipped open the top folder. "The transcript is right here. You'll see that he asks for clothes, weapons, ID, that kind of thing. Plus a trace on the Stony Man computer relating to a man called Latta."

"Where does he want this stuff? Belgium?"

"In the diplomatic bag to Brussels, yes, sir."

"You're telling me the kidnappers took him all the way to Europe?"

"That's the way it looks."

"And he escaped and wants to hit back at this guy Latta?"

"You know Bolan much better than me," O'Reilly said tactfully.

Brognola sighed. "Don't I ever! He didn't say *why* he was snatched?"

"No, I, uh, don't believe he knows. Maybe he wants to find out."

"That figures. Is that trace in hand?"

O'Reilly nodded. "I called Kurtzman at Stony Man as soon as the signal was decoded."

"The tackle, too?"

"Requisitioned from . . . reliable suppliers."

Brognola was satisfied. He knew better than to ask who those suppliers were. Official requests for the kind of gear and documents Bolan wanted would keep the wires red-hot if the Pentagon, or Langley, knew who the stuff was for. But there were always shortcuts, and Frank would know them. Brognola himself knew that his name—maybe even what looked like his signature—and the full authority of the Justice Department would be invoked to get the Executioner's goodies accepted as diplomatic bag material. But he didn't say anything about that, either.

Among professionals, some things were better left unsaid.

He changed the subject. "These damned photographic plates that Zulowski sent—any progress there?"

O'Reilly shrugged. "There's an image, something recorded in the emulsion. But like you said, it's meaningless. Whatever way the darkroom boys handle it, they come up with the same scene. It could be a shot of electrons bombarding a neutron, a supernova exploding fifty million years ago, or just the interference on a TV screen. You tell me."

"Don't give me that crap, Frank," Brognola growled. "You know as well as I do that Zulowski photographed the pages of a list. Names and addresses, thumbnail biogs, connections. In some way these pictures have been, well, coded *visually*. What we have to do is find the key."

"He was killed outside the post office," O'Reilly said. "Maybe he was on his way to send us that key. Maybe he *had* sent it. The Company's Brussels resident went down. There was nothing on the body."

"Well, there wouldn't be, would there? If he didn't mail whatever it was, the killers would have taken it off him."

"Zulowski was shot from a rooftop across the street," O'Reilly objected, "just like the woman witness at the police station here. There wasn't time for the killer to get anywhere near the body."

"Well, if he'd mailed it, we should have had it by now," the Fed replied irritably. "And we don't. But it has to be located. This operation is too sensitive and important to start over."

O'Reilly scratched his head. "Yeah, but—"

The phone rang.

Brognola grabbed the handset. The call lasted two minutes, and during it he uttered only three monosyllables. He replaced the receiver, turning to O'Reilly.

"That was the result of your trace. Fraser Latta. He's a laundryman for the international Mob. Converts their loot into legitimate business channels through connections in Switzerland, Liechtenstein, the Bahamas, you name it. Legally clean as far as the FBI, the IRS and the other countries are concerned. But he's neck-deep in crime all the same. It's just that there's no proof. Big operator, too. Manhattan penthouse, ranch in Apple Valley, apartments in Paris, London and Bonn, a villa in Palermo, Sicily." Brognola paused for effect. "And a country estate near the Luxembourg border, in Belgium."

O'Reilly whistled. "Are you thinking what I'm thinking?"

"I'd say it was crystal clear," Brognola nodded. "Zulowski acquires a list of names that would blow a big-time Mafia operation wide open. He's wasted in Luxembourg before he can let us in on the method he used to transmit the evidence. Then Bolan is kidnapped and taken to Europe, to a place not a hundred miles from Luxembourg. By a guy who's a big wheel in the Mob's commercial activities. How do you read that, Frank?"

"The Bolan grab and the Zulowski mission are connected?" the security chief offered.

"Bingo. And?"

O'Reilly plucked at his lower lip. "It bothers me that they could track Bolan, but I'd say they figured he *was* on a mission. The same mission as Zulowski. And they snatched him because they hoped he could tell them something...something they couldn't get out of Zulowski himself."

"Right. And as they already got back the list, the original, they must've known he'd sent copies here—"

"And they wanted those," O'Reilly cut in. "Or...No, maybe they knew he'd sent them some unusual way, and they hoped Bolan would know how. That he could tip them off to, well, what you call the key to his visual code."

"Yeah," Brognola said slowly. "I'd say that's part of it. But it doesn't entirely stack up. *How* would they know he'd sent them a crazy way? And if they did, why wouldn't they know what key he used? This doesn't tell us one damned thing more, not about the key, not about the reason for Bolan's kidnapping!"

"What do you aim to do?"

The Fed thought for a moment, drumming his fingers on the top of his desk. Then a sly smile spread over his face. "I'll tell you what we'll do, Frank," he said. "We'll make a connection ourselves. Bolan's over there, right where the action is. He asked us to send him matériel in the diplomatic bag. We'll go one better. We'll send it by courier. And the courier will carry a message too, what you might call a briefing."

"You mean...?"

"I mean he's there, he's at the center of this mystery. He can have all the help he wants—but let him solve it himself! As of now, Frank, Mack Bolan *is* on a mission."

The desk intercom buzzed. "What is it?" Brognola called.

"The technician from the photo-analysis lab is here, sir," the receptionist's voice replied. "He says they discovered what those plates from Brussels are about."

"Thanks. Have him come in."

The middle-aged man who appeared a moment later was short and balding, with a thin face and heavy black-rimmed spectacles. He wore a pleased smile. "Do you know what a hologram is, Mr. Brognola?"

8

"A hologram," Colonel Stefan Heller told Mack Bolan, "is in effect a photograph in three dimensions obtained without the use of conventional lenses. Its advantage—or disadvantage in your particular case—is that the finished plate is useless without the original means of producing it."

Bolan cleared his throat. "I'm familiar with the general proposition, but you'll have to be a little more specific, Colonel."

"Very well, I'll start with the basics."

The two men were sitting on stools at an optical bench in a top-secret laboratory hidden inside an old hill fort near Malmédy, which had once been part of Belgium's forward defenses against Hitler's armies.

Bolan, briefed, supplied with weapons, money and papers for his cover identity as Mike Belasko by the courier from Washington, had driven down from Liège that morning. The fort, perched on a spur that projected from one of the Ardennes escarpments, was one of the most closely guarded of all NATO research centers. Heller had been a professor of optics attached to the Belgian State University at Mons before he was made its director general. He was a short man, compactly built, with immaculately waved silver hair and gold-rim spectacles. He looked—Bolan thought, trying hard to concentrate—so much like a character actor from central casting playing a professor that it was disconcerting.

"For holography," Colonel Heller was saying, "you have to have the laser. You are perhaps familiar with the laser, Mr. Belasko?"

"You could almost say intimate," replied the warrior, who had once nearly been carved up by one in a KGB-controlled prison in Sofia.

"So. Then you will know that the laser is an exceptionally brilliant light source, produced by the stimulation of crystals or gases, in which all the waves are, so to speak, 'in step.' It's what we call coherent light.

"Holography," the Belgian continued, settling now into his lecturer's groove, "is a method of photography employing this light. Only instead of using a lens to record a focused image on the sensitized plate, we record simply a pattern of interference between two separate beams of coherent light directed at the image."

"Directed at whatever is being photographed."

"Yes. We record a pattern of interference, I say, as one might record the pattern produced when two stones are dropped into a pool and the widening circles of ripples intermingle."

"Okay, but I—"

"Patience, young man!" Heller reproved. "To make a hologram, we set up the object to be photographed and shine our laser beam at it. But not directly! Oh, no. We shine it through some semitranslucent medium that both reflects and refracts...a piece of half-silvered mirror, for instance, a fragment of frosted glass. Even a sheet of plastic."

"Plastic?"

"Plastic."

Bolan reckoned he was getting half the Mons third-year optics course free.

"Now what happens? Half the light penetrates the medium and goes on to illuminate the subject. And the remainder is reflected back toward the light source, where we allow it to fall on the photographic plate. The light beam that goes on through to illuminate the subject also makes its way back to the photographic plate eventually. And it's the recording of the interference between these two halves of the original beam that creates the hologram."

"So what's the effect?" Bolan asked. "On the plate, I mean."

"When it's developed, it reveals what seems to be a meaningless blur. But wait!" Heller raised an admonitory finger. "Ordinarily we would only have to shine the original light source—the laser—at this blur, and presto! We would see the original subject again in three dimensions.

"But our labs have been working on a new process, developed especially for high-security operations. Using this new system, you must have the original piece of glass that you first used to split the laser beam, in order to re-divide it. The divided laser beam is then aimed at the holographic negative to recreate the three-dimensional image. Without that piece of glass—or whatever you used—the negative will remain an indecipherable blur."

He slipped off the stool and bounded across to his desk and opened a wide, shallow drawer, taking out what appeared to be an ordinary glass photo plate about six inches by four inches and handed it to Bolan. "I'll give you a demonstration."

Bolan glanced at the plate, which looked like a close-up of a piece of granite or a pattern formed by an asymmetric kaleidoscope, a random assembly of different specks.

"That," Heller said, "is a hologram." He bustled about between the desk and a series of work tables ranged along one wall. "Now I'll bring it back to life for you."

He dragged across a heavy box on a tripod, fitted with two dials and a row of switches. Then he plugged a cable into an electrical outlet and attached another cable projecting from the ventilation louvers on the steel side of the box to a complex framework screwed to the bench. In the frame he fixed a metal cylinder twenty inches long and five in diameter, from which protruded what looked like the hood on a camera lens. "This is a helium-neon laser," Heller explained. "Only a small one—thirty joules—since it's for demonstration. But watch what it can do."

He arranged a shabby, pockmarked mirror three feet away from the laser's output aperture, took back the hologram and slotted it into a groove prepared in the bench surface. He drew black curtains over the windows, handed Bolan dark glasses and killed the lights. A switch clicked. There was a brilliant blue-green flash from the bench, followed by a low humming noise.

Bolan saw a rose-colored fluorescence surrounding the laser cylinder, then a pencil of painfully intense crimson light pulsed from the aperture and lanced down the bench. Following its path above the polished wood, he sat transfixed.

Where there had been an empty space above the surface, he now saw a silver tray of coffee and liqueurs laid out—the shine on the bone china, a jeweled highlight lurking in the liquor. He reached out his hand and touched... nothing.

"I'm impressed."

"There's more." Heller switched on the lights, fetched a large picture frame from a corner and suspended it from a ceiling hook at the end of the bench. The glass inside the frame, like the smaller hologram Bolan had examined, displayed no more than a jumble of fragments. Yet once Heller had maneuvered the angle of the laser beam and reset some switches, the frame enclosed a perfect 3-D photo—a small-town street scene with striped awnings covering market stalls and cars parked by the entrance to an alley.

"Unbelievable!"

"It is, yes. But perhaps more than you realize, Mr. Belasko. Come here and look down that alley."

The warrior whistled in amazement. Moving to his right, around the frame, craning to see down the narrow lane in the photo, he found that he could see the radiator grill of an additional car, invisible before.

Heller laughed. "Yes, you really do 'see around corners' with coherent light. We have a video demonstration. A man stands in front of his desk and you can step to one side and peer around to see the gun he'd hidden behind his back! There's a big transparency that works in ordinary light. Hang it before a window and you see a life-size portrait of a lady, apparently standing solid in space!"

"Remarkable," Bolan said, "but as to a document...?"

"A document? But the same principle applies. A secret document—a blueprint for example—could only be deciphered if the decoder knew precisely how it was made. Suppose the laser light had been refracted and reflected via a sheet of frosted glass. The hologram could only be turned back into blueprint by shining the same light at it through the same sheet of glass, in exactly the same position. It would be very useful for a spy!''

"Yeah," the Executioner said dryly, "you could be right. You're telling me that it would remain indecipherable unless you had that same piece of glass and shone the same light—''

"Exactly."

"And if the glass was lost or broken?"

"If our new system was employed, the hologram would remain a meaningless blur. Even if it fell into enemy hands, there'd be no way he could turn it back into a blueprint without the glass.''

Bolan sighed. "That's our problem. An agent used this new type of holography to copy secret papers. We have the holograms, but the refracting medium was to come by a different route. Now the agent is dead and the medium is lost. If only Zulowski—''

"Zulowski!" the Colonel exclaimed. "René Zulowski? A dark gentleman about thirty? Always wearing sunglasses?''

"I guess so."

"But he was here!" The Belgian was surprised. "One week ago. He had come to see me to ask if he could borrow the helium-neon laser for a half hour.''

"He had to have copied the documents here in this lab.''

"Undoubtedly."

"Were you with him while he used the apparatus?"

Heller shook his head. "Alas, no. I had work elsewhere, so I left him in the labs. And when I came back he was gone. But at least I can tell you what wavelength is the light you must use—when you find your medium.''

"Yeah. When and if. Tell me how Zulowski was on laser-borrowing terms with an organization like this." Bolan waved around the high-tech optical installation.

Colonel Heller coughed. "It was, uh, something of a personal matter. I owed a favor to this commercial attaché in one of the EEC Commissions in Brussels, and it seems that the wife of this gentleman's cousin and Mr. Zulowski's sister were at Geneva—" He shrugged.

"I get the picture. You don't just do military research here, do you?" Bolan asked, curious.

"By no means. There are implications in molecular biology. We're working on a system to translate books into international computer language. Rinaldi in Milan is using lasers to analyze the shock waves surrounding supersonic jetliners. And so on."

"I have to thank you for your help, colonel."

"It is nothing. A pleasure. It's curious, just the same, that you should be the second person to inquire about this Zulowski."

Bolan halted on his way to the door. "The second?"

"Some days ago another gentleman was asking, an industrialist from Cologne, named Latta. He was very upset when we were unable to assist him."

BOLAN'S RENTED Alfa Romeo was approaching a sharp curve less than a mile from the NATO installation.

The road was zigzagging down the escarpment below the guarded perimeter, and he intended to downshift to third. But although the warrior pumped hard with his right foot, the sports car refused to slow.

He pulled up on the hand brake.

Nothing. He had no brakes.

Bolan could think of only one thing: sabotage.

He double clutched, and slammed the short lever into third. The Alfa slowed enough for him to wrestle it around the curve, the open body canting over, the tires screeching.

But below, the road dropped like an elevator—a short, steep section terminating in another 180-degree curve so acute and with such an inverse slope on the surface that even with brakes most drivers would have needed two bites at it.

Despite the engine compression, the weight of the car pushed the speed up almost to 60 mph again. Double clutching once more, Bolan attempted to force the lever across and down into second. The engine screamed in protest as the needle swept into the tach's red line; a hideous noise grated from the gearbox, but the lever remained shuddering in neutral. He tried again, but it still refused to engage. And the hairpin turn was dead ahead.

With a curse, he banged it back into third and wrenched at the wheel. Lurching, the Alfa Romeo ran out of road at the foot of the grade. As the tail swung out and struck the bank, the tires howled broadside across the pavement. The roadster burst through a stone parapet backward, rose into the air and somersaulted down the hillside in a shower of stones. It smashed into bare earth, bounced onto another road below, shattered a second stone wall and finally crunched to a halt on its back among the rocks.

Bolan had been thrown clear with the first impact.

Bruised, shaken, but otherwise unhurt, he crouched behind a boulder, peering through the yellow dust cloud eddying up from the slope. The Beretta 93-R pistol sent to him by Brognola's courier was in his right hand.

A few pebbles still rattled down the incline. Wind soughed through treetops farther down the hill. But no other sounds were audible.

Rock splinters suddenly stung his cheek, as a heavy-caliber slug whined off the boulder. Bolan was flat on his face behind the huge stone before the whip-crack of the power rifle high up on the escarpment reached his ears.

9

Bolan located the marksman after the third shot rang out. The guy was standing openly, almost insolently, beside a dwarf pine tree on the edge of the escarpment, a sinister figure silhouetted against the sky.

All three rounds had been uncomfortably close.

Bolan presented himself deliberately to draw fire, darting out from behind the boulder and diving back. Before he took any action himself he wanted to check out the killer's weapon.

The bullet gouged a channel in the rock two inches in front of the warrior's foot. By the time the report reached his ears, he was back behind the boulder with his eye to the fissure through which he'd first glimpsed the gunman.

The guy was breaking the long-barreled shooter, feeding shells into the breech. His weapon was loaded like a shotgun, so it had to be a magazineless sporting rifle, double-barreled: there'd been no time for a reload between the last two rounds. The rifle was firing heavy knockdown rounds, probably .30-caliber softnose material. It was, Bolan estimated, around four hundred yards away. With the scope, it could be as deadly at half a mile.

In other words, the killer was free to go wherever he liked, as openly as he liked, and keep Bolan totally pinned down, unless and until he came within range of the Beretta—which, at this distance was pretty well useless.

The Executioner was in a tough situation. There was nothing but a bare slope of shale for twenty yards on both sides of the boulder, and the jumble of smaller rocks beyond that offered little cover, especially if the sniper chose to move lower down the escarpment.

A steep bank rose above the curve where the Alfa Romeo had burst through the parapet, but it was separated from the boulder by forty or fifty feet of loose stone as devoid of cover as the ground.

Below there was bedrock until the next loop of road and the ditch, beyond which was the wrecked car.

Could a desperate man make the bank, ditch or the battered convertible in twelve to fifteen seconds?

No way.

So what was his next move? The killer wasn't going to wait on top of the escarpment until night fell and allow the warrior to get away. He wasn't going to wait until the early shift left the NATO installation and took the road home.

There were plenty of trees below the Alfa, an ocean of trees washing up to the foot of the escarpment one hundred yards on either side of the bare hillside where Bolan was trapped.

He had to make it to the trees before the killer did.

Otherwise all the cards would stay in the gunner's hand. There were several minor ridges between the boulder and the foot of the escarpment, which would offer the sniper cover. Invisible behind these, he could reach a position from which he could fire at the Executioner...from either side. And once he lost sight of him,

Bolan wouldn't know which side of the boulder would keep him out of range.

He moved slightly, advancing a leg and a shoulder beyond the rock buttress. The slug splatted against the stone surface, showering him with tiny fragments.

Once.

On hands and knees, he moved into view for an instant on the far side of the boulder.

The sniper held his fire, so Bolan tried again on the other side. Nothing.

Bolan cursed. The guy was smart—he was wise to the stratagem—and the warrior didn't know whether he'd used the time to feed back a shell and replace the round he'd used.

The killer was making his move. Bolan watched him step down from the lip of the escarpment and tread warily along a path traversing the near-vertical face, the rifle's point of balance cradled in the gunner's left hand.

He made the top of the slope, slid twenty yards in a cloud of dust and pebbles, and approached the first of the ground swells in the hillside. The lower half of the sniper's body was hidden from view as he approached the crest.

Would he take advantage of the cover, duck down and make for one of the tree belts, leaving Bolan to guess which? Or would he *pretend* to do that, stay prone right where he was, and gun the warrior down when he made his break?

The sniper did neither. He breasted the rise and walked slowly down, across a rock outcrop, through a patch of brushwood and into a dip before the next rise. This time he did disappear.

Gazing intently through the rock fissure, Bolan weighed the pros and cons. The fact that he could no longer see the killer didn't necessarily mean that the guy wouldn't see *him* if he made a break—particularly if he was waiting for Bolan to do just that.

Attack was the best method of defense, not that this was attack in a military sense. But psychologically? It was worth a try.

As far as he could see through the crack in the rock, he estimated the farthest distance the rifleman could have traveled in either direction since he vanished from view. Then vectoring in on the boulder from those two points, he drew a mental line from his hiding place to the road below that would give him the maximum protection from the rocky mass.

The Executioner holstered the Beretta in his quick-draw shoulder rig, took three quick steps away from the boulder and hurled himself down the stony slope, flinging himself against the hard surface of the outcrop, then going into a shoulder roll after a half dozen strides.

Two shots were fired immediately, then two more, moments later.

The first pair must have been fired when Bolan was on his feet, still partly hidden by the boulder, because they went wide. He was rolling when the next two blasted from the ridge.

They were close. One sent small stones tumbling a foot from his face; the second jarred his left leg as it tore the heel from his shoe. Then he dropped over the edge of the rock, bouncing down a grassy bank to sprawl on the road ten feet below.

He was safe, but only temporarily. For fifty or sixty yards he was covered by the bank from a marksman anyplace on the hillside above. As well, on each side there were hairpin curves, leading up on his left, down on the right. And from any position level with those he would be a sitting duck. He had merely exchanged one refuge for a wider one.

What he had to do now was reach the shelter of the trees below the Alfa before the gunman picked him off.

The Executioner crawled to the top of the bank, parting the grasses to scan the slant of hillside, and the trees bordering it, between him and the escarpment.

The sun disappeared behind a tower of clouds. A flight of small birds darted through the scrub higher up the slope. Nothing else moved.

Bolan's hawk eyes ranged slowly across the terrain from left to right, alert for a telltale swaying branch, a shape that moved behind a screen of leaves, a shadow behind a rise. The sun reemerged, splashing the trees with light, then vanished again behind another cloud bank. But in that moment, for the second time, a flash of light reflected from the sniper's scope and betrayed the killer's position: on Bolan's left, under the trees, perhaps two hundred yards away.

Now that he knew where to look, the warrior could see the man stealthily advancing downhill, partially screened by bushes. In two minutes, maybe three, he'd be level with the hairpin curves, Bolan locked in his sights...and still out of effective range.

The warrior's mind raced. While he deliberated, a puff of warm wind blew the sharp smell of gasoline his way. He flicked a glance across the road and saw that fuel was dripping from the ruptured tank of the Alfa Romeo. The shale beneath the capsized rear end was dark with the spilled liquid and the air above vibrated as the gas vaporized.

The tank was between the rear wheels, just ahead of the suspension arms. To reach the ground, therefore, the leaking gas had to percolate through the crumpled tank and out past the lid. So the tail would be full of an explosive mixture, vapor mixed with air.

Bolan unleathered the Beretta.

More than once in his combat career he'd ignited spilled gasoline by firing slugs off a hard surface to strike a spark. He squeezed off two experimental rounds, but there were no flints in the crumbling shale and the slugs buried themselves in the weathered shale.

He felt in his pocket and drew out a king-sized box of matches. Then sliding down the bank, he crawled out across the road until he could just see that sector of the wood where he'd located the gunman.

Two shots cracked out with frightening rapidity. Bolan drew back a microsecond before the pavement was pitted where he had stood an instant before.

Barely out of the gunman's sight, allowing a couple of feet extra for the killer to move farther downhill, the Executioner struck a match and flung it toward the wreck.

The breeze killed the flame and blew the matchstick back toward the Executioner. He tried again, and again, but had the same result.

Bolan attempted splitting a match, wedging a second into the split, and then a third, to gain more weight so that the flame would carry. No good.

Finally he slid the matchbox one-third open, so that the phosphor-impregnated heads were exposed. He removed three more matches, scraped them into flame and held them together beneath the open end of the box. The entire box erupted into a mini-fireball that hissed like a steam valve. Bolan wound up like a man on the mound and pitched.

The flaming matchbox arrowed across the road, hit the side of the wrecked convertible and dropped to the gasoline-soaked shale beneath.

The thump of the igniting fuel was swamped by a cracking shellburst of sound as the volatile mixture inside the trunk exploded, flaming debris spewing outward. A curved steel panel scythed across the road to plunge into the bank ten feet from the Executioner; a blazing seat cushion landed at his feet.

Within seconds the rear end of the Alfa was a seething inferno, and it was then that the incandescent mass produced the result Bolan had hoped for.

The spare tire, then those on the rear wheels, caught fire, billowing black smoke into the air.

The wind that had foiled Bolan's initial efforts with the matches now worked in his favor, rolling the dense cloud toward him and up the bank.

Screened by the choking smoke, he sprinted across the road, ran down the slope and in among the trees.

10

The tires burned for a long time, the black smoke boiling across the road and up the hillside. The flames licking the rest of the wreck gradually dwindled and died. Bolan crouched in the fork of an oak tree and waited.

The sun had vanished behind the escarpment, and the light was already beginning to thicken before the smoke screen thinned enough for him to see the two curves and the woods on either side. So far there'd been no further sign of the rifleman, but Bolan sensed that he wouldn't be far away. His orders were to kill; he wasn't going to quit until he had relocated his target.

Bolan wasn't about to quit either; he didn't like people tampering with his car and shooting at him. Right now there wasn't anywhere he *could* go. The warrior was savvy enough to know it was in the cards that the killer would have stashed buddies farther down the road—just in case he should try to escape that way.

So he waited and watched.

While he was waiting, he allowed himself to review the courier's briefing in Liège. At first he'd been as surprised as hell. Brognola was exacting "payment" for the help Bolan had requested. He was asking Bolan to get involved in a mission that any half-assed rookie spook could have handled: an attempt to backtrack on an operation some other agent had already screwed up.

Then, when the earnest little courier had pointed out that the search for the missing hologram factor was connected with the Executioner's own kidnapping, which explained Latta and the girl's insistence on systems of communications, he'd been mollified.

Obviously he'd been grabbed because the conspirators figured he was *already* involved in the Zulowski operation.

When he learned the significance of the list—and the Mafia angle—Bolan couldn't turn his back on this mission.

"It's rather more than a list, actually," the courier had said. "What we have here is a report, specially compiled for a man named Vito Maccione, one of the Mob's most important and ruthless capos."

Bolan nodded. "I know Maccione. He was deported from the States in 1967 and now lives in Cologne, West Germany, where he hopes to penetrate industry in the Ruhr."

"That's just the beginning," the courier said somberly. "This report is in fact a listing of all the European industries, cartels, companies and multinational subsidiaries that the Mafia intends to infiltrate by means of takeovers, front organizations and, in many cases, blackmail of stockholders."

Bolan whistled. "And Fraser Latta's the financial genius who's going to make it legal?"

"You got it. If it's successful, the plan will give the Mob effective control of the major part of electronics, telecommunications, aerospace accessories and armaments, among other things."

"That's heavy-duty," Bolan said.

"Such a concentration of power would gravely compromise the stability of the Middle East if one country in need of arms was played off against another—guns to the highest bidder. It could be used as a lever for extortion on a global scale if, as Maccione intends, threats were made to let sensitive enterprises into Soviet or Chinese hands."

"Yeah," Bolan said. "And if they employ the usual strong-arm persuasion—digging up dirt, blackmailing people in key positions, making threats—it could lead to an increase in crime that would make Europe look like Chicago in the days of Prohibition."

The courier was pacing up and down the esplanade overlooking the river. Although it was a warm spring day and striped parasols shaded the shirt-sleeved drinkers at a sidewalk café across the street, he was wearing a belted trench coat and a wide-brimmed hat. He looked, Bolan thought, like a junior bank clerk kidding himself he was Philip Marlowe. It was difficult to believe that anyone could take him seriously as an intelligence agent. "The report," the courier announced, "details the methods to be used for each takeover, the financial clout already deployed in the target industries, and most importantly the names of the moles—the suborned department chiefs and financial advisers in each company who will secretly aid the plan."

"We have a copy of this report, but we can't read it, right?"

"That is correct. Zulowski was once a safecracker. He stole the original from Maccione's place in Cologne. Before they repossessed it and gunned him down, he'd copied each page and sent it to Mr. Brognola in the form of a hologram. The effect is analogous optically to that of a telephone scrambler."

"And all I have to do is find out what he used to make the hologram so that the photos can be unscrambled?"

"Exactly. Did you know Zulowski?"

Bolan shook his head.

"He was a good man." Thick-lensed spectacles glinted in the sun as the courier looked Bolan in the eye. "I don't need to tell you," he said, "that such a document is vital to our own as well as to the European governments if we're to prevent a worldwide Mafia tyranny."

"I get the picture."

"Let us hope so...literally," the courier replied.

A few minutes later, having fed the Executioner another ration of background from Brognola, he hopped onto a bus heading for the railroad station and vanished from sight.

Later, alone in his tree in the Ardennes, Bolan examined the implications of the courier's story.

The Mob must have been breathing down Zulowski's neck: they knew he'd made holograms of the stolen report, and where. Otherwise Latta would never have been at the NATO base asking questions.

They knew he'd dispatched the holograms stateside, and they must have also known that he hadn't yet sent the complementary medium through which they'd been shot. But they didn't know what medium he'd used. And because they couldn't catch up with Zulowski in time to force him to tell them, they'd killed him to stop him from sending it.

It was then that Bolan had been kidnapped—mistakenly—in the hope that he was part of the mission and could give them the information they needed.

Too bad.

And because he escaped when he did, they still didn't know whether or not he knew the secret of the holograms.

They could, of course, have picked him up again easily enough, simply by keeping watch on Heller's optical research station. But how had Latta gained access to that ultrasecret installation? Because there were Mafia contacts inside?

That made sense. Otherwise, how could someone have been on hand to sabotage the Alfa Romeo? And how would they have known that Bolan was armed only with a handgun?

A lot of questions went unanswered, such as who was the mole? Heller himself?

At first that seemed the obvious choice. But if he was, why wouldn't he simply have stuck with Zulowski when he made the holograms and called up Latta to eliminate him then and there? In any case, why tell Bolan that Latta had been there?

That cap didn't fit after all. Just the same, the Executioner made a mental note to ask Brognola's office to run a trace on Colonel Stefan Heller.

He'd have to take care of that some other time. Right now there was a more urgent question demanding an answer.

Where was the sniper? How long would it be before he revealed himself? And was he still hunting?

Suddenly Bolan saw him. He was standing at the left-hand end of the ditch, staring fixedly at the gutted convertible. One moment the landscape had been deserted; the next, there he was, the twin-barrel rifle slung across his back, a mini-Uzi machine pistol gripped in his hands.

Bolan's right hand was raw and blistered, scorched by the flaming box of matches. But he managed to wrap the palm around the butt of his Beretta, wincing slightly as the burned flesh of the index finger contacted the cold, steel trigger.

The killer was on the move. Unhurriedly he crossed the road and vanished among the trees.

Bolan hesitated. Should he drop to ground level to give himself the same maneuverability as the gunman? Or should he capitalize on concealment and a wider range of visibility and stay where he was . . . at the risk of finding himself cornered if the guy was smart enough to flush him out first?

The question prompted another. The rifleman had orders to kill, but how could he be sure that Bolan was still around, that he hadn't penetrated the woods and made a cross-country escape?

The answer to that one came fast.

Away to the Executioner's left, hidden somewhere in a denser part of the wood, he heard an unmistakable sound—the crackling rasp of a voice issuing from a shortwave radio receiver.

He couldn't make out the words, and he couldn't hear the killer's reply, but it didn't take an Einstein to read the score.

There *was* a backup team somewhere farther down the road, and they were telling the hunter no, the quarry hadn't passed that way.

Bolan balanced mobility against the long view, and time and motion came out on top.

At close quarters like this, his Beretta was accurate over a much longer range than a mini-Uzi. But within its 150-yard killground, the little SMG's 1200 rounds-per-minute deathblast was something that the smart fighter was wise to avoid.

Bolan dropped silently from the tree onto a bed of last year's dead leaves. He ran for the bare, noiseless earth behind a thick clump of evergreen bushes and lowered himself into a combat crouch, the muzzle of the Beretta questing right and left as his steely gaze swept the complex of trunks, branches and fresh green leaves between his hiding place and the section of woods where he'd last seen the man with the Uzi.

There was a heavy and oppressive silence beneath the trees—the evening air seemed suddenly to have grown damp and clammy. Clouds of insects drifted like smoke in the gathering dusk.

A dry twig snapped, shattering the forest calm. The noise sounded as deafening as a cannon shot. A startled bird flapped heavily away among the treetops, and there were rustlings in the undergrowth near the Executioner's screen of bushes.

He crouched lower, his eyes straining to pierce the gloom for a movement, a shadow, a swaying bough not caused by the occasional gusts of wind that stirred the foliage.

It was impossible in these conditions to estimate with any accuracy the distance or the precise direction of a noise that didn't belong. But Bolan guessed the twig had been snapped around sixty or seventy yards away, still off to his left but deeper into the woods.

Another dry branch snapped, much nearer this time.

Clearly the killer's woodcraft was not up to the standard of his long-distance sniping technique.

Bolan lowered himself to the forest floor and eeled his way toward a patch of thorny undergrowth that was less than waist high—the last place an inexperienced stalker would expect a big man to be hiding.

Breathing shallowly beneath the lowest strands of spicy scrub, Bolan waited....

It was five minutes before he saw the stalker, and then it was only a fleeting glance, a glimpse between two close-growing trees of a miniature glade, perhaps forty yards away. But it was enough for the warrior to register the fact that the rifle was still slung across the man's back, that his right hand held the mini-Uzi by its pistol grip, leaving the left free to push aside and hold back branches that might block his way or swish noisily as he soft-footed past.

Bolan noticed too that the subgun was fitted with the short, 20-round box magazine. Which meant—in theory at least—that at full blast the weapon would be out of ammunition after a single second's continuous firing.

Once more it was the Executioner's strategy to draw the killer's fire, then move in while he reloaded. But the Uzi's deathstream wasn't to be underestimated: that one-second burst could rip the human body in two. So the fire, if possible, had to be drawn to where Bolan wasn't.

His mind raced, trying to think of a suitable decoy.

The killer was drawing nearer. Every few seconds now Bolan could distinguish a stealthy footfall among the thickly growing stalks and stems to his left. He held his breath, listening to the thump of his own heart against the earth.

And something else—faint but unmistakable, a high-pitched whine that was abruptly killed.

It was something called negative feedback, generated by badly-adjusted microphones, radios that were clumsily tuned... and short-range high-frequency transceivers?

In these circumstances, coming from behind the Executioner and to his right, it could only mean one thing. The rifleman had called up a confederate, and now there was a second killer approaching Bolan from the rear.

11

The second player was a better woodsman than the guy with the rifle. Although Bolan strained with every fiber of his being to catch an indication, a hint, an echo of his approximate location, his ears relayed nothing but an occasional furtive slither from the part of the woods where he'd last seen the first gunner.

Suddenly the shadows beneath the trees were filled with whispering. The breeze had freshened and branches high above swayed, but the low, muttering voices were not figments of the warrior's imagination. By some acoustic freak of tree trunks and irregularities in the ground, they seemed to come from all around him, a sinister murmur that swelled over the distant crackle of flames still licking parts of the burned-out Alfa Romeo.

But Bolan knew those voices were much nearer than the wreck: the killers were in low-pitched radio liaison, secure in the knowledge that if their quarry did happen to be near enough to home in on one of the speakers and open fire, he would instantly transform himself into a prime target for the other.

The hell with it. Bolan had played a passive role long enough. As a combat veteran he craved action, and he knew from long experience that the soldier acting first had the advantage.

Okay, since he was aware, if only roughly, of his enemies' positions—and they knew nothing of his—he would use that advantage, stir the pot and see what floated to the surface.

Immediately beyond the patch of thorny scrub there was a shallow depression buttressed on one side by the gnarled roots of a wide-boled oak. Bolan readied his prone body, tensing each muscle like a coiled spring, the Beretta in his right hand.

Then he called in a loud voice, "Hey! Over here!"

He moved the instant the last syllable left his mouth, rolling violently out from under the spines and into the depression. The sounds of his displacement were drowned in a savage blast of gunfire. The man with the mini-Uzi was no more than twenty yards away, his whole body shuddering with the multiple concussions as the subgun hosed half a magazine of 9 mm hornets into the scrub.

Ripped stems and leaves were still in midair when Bolan, lying on his back in the hollow with the Beretta held in both hands above his head, triggered his own first salvo.

He heard a smothered curse, a threshing among the bushes where the gunman had been hiding, then the sound of a heavy fall. Three shots from the Beretta had smashed into the guy's shoulder, crippling him but not taking him completely out of play. From the ground the wounded killer blazed the remainder of the Uzi's magazine one-handed through the undergrowth toward the hollow. At the same time, since the Executioner had revealed his position with that first burst, four separate rounds from a heavy-caliber revolver reverberated from a thicket of saplings fifty yards on the other side of the depression.

But Bolan was no longer in the hollow. He was behind the broad trunk of the oak, pulse hammering and breath heaving with the sudden exertion.

With the Beretta in 3-shot mode, he choked out a second message of death, special delivery among the roots of the bushes where the rifleman had fallen. This time he scored. A body flopped into the bushes and then lay still.

Targeting on the Beretta's muzzle-flashes in the gloom, the second guy pumped four more .45 ACP boattails across the killground. White marks scarred the trunk of the oak tree as strips of bark flew wide, but the Executioner had dodged around to the far side... and now the decoy strategy paid off. For the second killer had already emptied his clip. The warrior had counted the shots.

He stepped out into the open, stitching the remaining slugs from his weapon in a lethal figure eight across the stand of saplings. Two of the young trees split at the base and careened outward, allowing a heavy body to fall facedown to the forest floor.

Bolan reholstered his weapon and walked across to the screen of bushes where the first man had dropped. The earth was black with blood from the guy's smashed arm and the gory pulp that had been his face. The double-barreled rifle was still slung across his back, but a small transceiver clipped to his lapel had been shattered.

The mini-Uzi was lying nearby. Bolan felt the dead man's jacket pockets and found a spare clip. Since he hadn't expected a shooting match when he left his hotel in Liège, he wasn't carrying extra ammunition for the Beretta. He picked up the SMG and slammed home a full clip.

A crackle of static broke the forest silence. Bolan stepped over to the second man and rolled the body over.

The rifleman's features had been obliterated, but the warrior knew this one: it was the first perimeter guard he'd spoken to on the Latta estate. White splinters of bone pricked through the red ruin of his chest, but the transceiver above was undamaged.

"I'm asking you again," the voice behind the grill complained. "Did you waste the bastard?"

Bolan unclipped the transceiver, thumbed the Send button and growled, "Yeah. It's over."

"Okay," the voice replied. "Wait by the roadside. We'll pick you up in the heap. Three minutes."

Bolan walked out of the wood and crouched behind the gutted Alfa. It was almost dark. The night air was bitter with the odors of burned rubber and plastics. Tongues of flame still licked occasionally at the mangled remains of the engine, sending whiffs of oily smoke across the hillside.

Three cars on the road from the escarpment looped down toward the trees, their headlights gleaming against the oncoming night. Most of the NATO personnel drove home to the city on the far side of the bluff, but a few lived in villages between the research station and the German frontier. Bolan let them pass: the people he was waiting for would be coming the other way.

Soon he saw light flickering between the trees. A car was climbing uphill on the far side of the woods. The headlight beams swung around the tight curve on the right of the ditch and slowed, approaching the wreck.

A voice called out, but Bolan stayed where he was, out of sight. The car stopped twenty yards away.

A door opened, actuating a courtesy light that illuminated the interior and revealed three men. The guy in the passenger seat got out, stared toward the Alfa and called, "Weber! Ghinzani! Where the hell are you?"

Bolan stood up behind the charred chassis of the convertible, holding the mini-Uzi at waist height, his scorched right hand around the pistol grip, his left grasping the grooves behind the gun's stubby muzzle to minimize climb.

"You'll find the bodies in the woods!" he shouted and squeezed the subgun's trigger.

Bolan had no compunction. These men were cold-blooded killers, members of one of the most ruthless and callous organizations the world had ever known. Five gunners had been sent out with orders to shoot him down. Mercy wasn't a word that figured in the Mob vocabulary. Bolan, on the other hand, had once been known as Sergeant Mercy, because of his compassion for Vietnamese civilians caught up in the horrors of war. It was not a quality he was prepared to extend to the Mafia.

But at least he would let his presence be known before he fired.

The gunner standing by the door of the sedan reacted. Flame blossomed from a gun in his hand, and a hail of lead caromed off the blackened steel spars of the wreck.

But the warrior's finger had already tightened on the trigger, and the Uzi's short, sharp burst crucified the gunman against the open door and shattered its window before he slid lifeless to the ground.

The driver smashed a hole in the windshield with the butt of his automatic and was hosing a concentrated deathstream toward the wreck within milliseconds of Bolan's opening blast.

The Executioner ducked behind the sportster's engine block as the high-tech slugs beat a harmless tattoo against the flame-scarred alloy. From the gravel on the far side of it, Bolan's second burst printed a tight pattern on the driver's chest.

The third man had hit the rear door at the first outbreak of shooting and dived to the ground on the other side of the car.

Bolan advanced into the open in a combat crouch. He heard scrabbling noises from behind the sedan, but he held his fire: he wanted the car usable, even with the windshield and one window missing.

He figured on tempting the last gunner out into a vulnerable position, waiting to see first which way the guy was going to attack.

The guy wasn't. He'd opted for running.

He was already on top of the bank, darting along the rock slope above the ditch, legs churning wildly as he raced back the way he had come.

Bolan fired the last few rounds in the Uzi's magazine when the gunner was well clear of his car, around forty yards away.

The fugitive spun around with a high-pitched scream, fell and rolled back to the road. But he was up again an instant later, staggering drunkenly, his shattered right arm hanging useless at his side. Sobbing for breath, he started once more to run.

The Executioner let him go.

After the roar of gunfire, the night seemed strangely silent. Bolan realized that the engine of the sedan was still quietly idling.

He dragged the dead killers to the side of the road, forced the crippled door shut, climbed behind the wheel and drove back toward the escarpment with his jacket slung over the bloodied driver's seat.

Nobody attempted to stop him on the way to the city. Windshields did get broken on country roads, and he junked the sedan before the streetlights were bright enough for someone to distinguish the bullet holes in the door.

He walked half a mile, picked up a cruising cab and went back to his hotel.

12

They came for him before he'd finished his breakfast coffee, two sturdy men of middle height flashing plasticized ID cards decorated with the black, red and yellow Belgian flag striped across the top left-hand corner.

"Police," the older of the men announced. "We must ask you to accompany us to the central station, Mr. Bolan. There are one or two questions the chief would like you to answer."

"The name is Belasko," Bolan said. "Mike Belasko, journalist. You want to see my papers?"

"There will be time for that later. It is less a question of identity than a matter of an abandoned Buick and four dead men in the woods below a certain NATO base."

Bolan's eyebrows rose. "And you think this Bolan can 'help you with your inquiries,' as they say? So why come to me? I think you better allow me to go to my room to get proof that I am who I say I am."

"No!" the older cop said sharply. The younger man unbuttoned his jacket and let it fall open enough to reveal the butt of the automatic that was tucked into his waistband.

"Come with us *now*." He jerked his head toward the door. Bolan shrugged and rose from the table.

A blue light flashed on the roof of the black Mercedes that was waiting at the foot of the steps leading down from the hotel entrance. A uniformed cop with an automatic rifle sat in the far corner of the rear seat; another man, apparently unarmed, was at the wheel.

Bolan was hustled in beside the guy with the gun, the younger plainclothesman got in beside him and closed the door and the older cop sat beside the driver. He picked a microphone from beneath the dashboard and spoke into it.

"Car D Danielle calling base. We're returning with the prisoner."

There was a reply, but Bolan couldn't make out the words. The driver gunned the engine and the Mercedes shot away from the curb, laying down a patch of rubber.

Ten minutes and one mile later, they were cruising northeast along the Quai St. Leonard, on the other side of the Meuse. Bolan, familiar with the city, asked, "Just where are we going? Police headquarters is between rue Maghin and rue St. Leonard."

"No talking," the older man snapped from the front seat.

"You already passed city hall and the immigration offices, but if we're—"

"Silence!"

Bolan gave up on conversation, but he'd been tipped. These guys weren't for real. And they should have been prepared to handle his questions. It stood to reason that he might know the city.

The whole setup was strictly amateurish. The flashing blue light on the roof, for instance, was the magnetic type clapped on by doctors when they needed to cut through traffic on an emergency call. On a genuine Belgian police car, the flasher would have been a fixture.

The car radio was nonstandard: the handset was shaped differently from the models equipping regular prowl cars in Liège. And no real police officer would refer to a man supposedly being brought in for routine questioning as "the prisoner."

A lot of routine was missing from the scripted dialogue they used getting him out of the hotel. But the real clincher was the use of his name.

No policeman in Liège—in Belgium, in the whole of Europe—could possibly know that a man named Mack Bolan was in town: he'd arrived secretly in the kidnappers' plane, with no papers, and had never appeared since his escape as anyone but Mike Belasko.

But Fraser Latta and his Mafia friends knew.

Bolan sighed. There were no options here, only one thing he could do, and he figured he could get away with it.

Bringing it down to basics, the operation was no more than a question of mathematics. That and the right road conditions, with traffic heavy enough and fast enough to keep the driver busy.

The man holding the automatic rifle had positioned it vertically, with the butt resting on the floor. The gun was a Kalashnikov AKM. The length of the assault rifle, Bolan knew, was thirty-four and a half inches. The Mercedes was the 16S version of the 2300 model, and the distance between the roof and the rear seat was…thirty-four and a half inches.

The width of the rear seat was fifty-five inches—fifty if you allowed for the intrusion of the elbow rests.

It followed that if the gunner brought the butt of the AKM up to seat height, he would be unable to wheel the rifle Bolan's way, because the muzzle would hit the roof. But if he contorted himself and swung it with the butt lower than that, by the time the barrel was horizontal the muzzle would be more than halfway across the width of the seat. And the Executioner was squeezed into the center.

In other words, as a weapon to menace Bolan while the car was moving and the rear doors closed, the Kalashnikov was useless.

Unprofessional, he noted, and inexperienced. They should have leveled the gun before Bolan got in, then shoved him into the corner with the muzzle boring into his gut. Either that or kept him covered all the time with the automatic that was still tucked into the waistband of the man on his other side.

With a team this stupid, Bolan reckoned he could act before the guy even whisked the gun out.

His opportunity came a few miles east of the city. They passed a long-distance expressway direction sign. White lettering on the green background indicated: E5-Aachen, Cologne: 2000 m. Just under two kilometers later, the Mercedes filtered right and sped up the ramp that connected with the turnpike leading to West Germany.

Bolan guessed he was on the way to the Mafia boss, Maccione, who lived in Cologne. He wondered how they aimed to get him across the border. Unconscious in the trunk?

He didn't intend to wait long enough to find out.

There were five lanes of traffic moving at the legal speed limit on the expressway, and the line of cars, buses and trucks moving up to join them were traveling slightly slower. A driver needed all the concentration he could command to slot himself neatly into the stream as it passed.

It was the opportunity Bolan had been waiting for. He made his play as the two roads converged.

Since he was unarmed—they'd frisked him expertly enough before they left the hotel—he thought it was safe to contrive a yawn, lean back in the seat and lace his hands behind his head. Safe enough, anyway, not to make them think he was planning anything.

They were suspicious nonetheless. "Put your hands down!" the man with the AKM snarled.

"Whatever you say," the warrior replied equably.

He unlinked the hands, then, with frogleg agility shot out his two arms, circled the necks of the men sitting on each side of him and brought their heads crashing together.

The impact wasn't enough to stun them, but it was the surprise element Bolan was counting on. Before they had recovered, his hands were freed—the left grabbing the wrist of the guy with the automatic, the right, bandaged because of the burns, jolting stiff-fingered into the uniformed cop's belly.

The gunner with the AKM doubled over, gasping for breath; the man with the automatic jerked the gun out of his waistband and tried to force Bolan's arm back so that the muzzle was pointing at his chest; the older guy in the front passenger seat whirled around, leaned over the seat back and reached for the Executioner.

Bolan slid right down in the seat until he was lying almost flat, using both hands now to haul the gunner, face upward, on top of him.

The driver cursed, wrestling the wheel as the struggling bodies lurched against his shoulder, sending the Mercedes veering into the faster traffic stream.

Somewhere among the tangle of limbs the gun went off. Bolan's steely grasp tightened, the muscles on his arms stood out. A second, and then a third shot rang out, deafeningly loud inside the sedan.

The man leaning into the back uttered a choking grunt, then blood poured from his gaping mouth onto the gun-

ner. The slugs that had cored his chest and ripped apart
his lungs smashed out between his shoulder blades and
shattered the windshield.

The driver braked fiercely, swearing again as the Mercedes slewed sideways with locked wheels. A flatbed
truck laden with crates of fruit caught the rear fender a
glancing blow and spun the car around. It came to rest
facing the wrong way on the soft shoulder in a litter of
apples, oranges and splintered wood.

Bolan, using all his strength, had heaved the gunner off
himself and onto the guy with the Kalashnikov. Now he
slid out from under, hit the door handle and dived out of
the vehicle.

He landed in a shoulder roll, leaped the low barrier and
slid down the grassy embankment of the expressway.

Three shots were fired, two from the automatic and
one from the AKM. None came anywhere near him.
Then the warrior was among the bushes that covered the
bottom of the slope.

Looking back, he saw traffic slowing to a halt all along
the road. Drivers were running toward the stalled Mercedes.

There was a dead man in there, and blood covered the
fragmented windshield. The motorists would think they'd
witnessed a daring prisoner escape. But already Bolan
could hear the hee-haw donkey bray of a genuine police
siren farther back along the expressway. The mafiosi
would have some explaining to do when the patrol car
arrived.

There were lessons to be learned from the encounter,
Bolan thought to himself as he trekked across two corn-
fields and emerged in a country lane.

It was clear now that the Mob would go to any lengths
to prevent Brognola and his analysts from deciphering

the hologram that enshrined the famous Mafia report—
even to the length of hiring the cheap goons that Bolan
had just bested. The risks of discovery in such a daring
and foolhardy operation were enough to underline the
urgency of the Mafia planning.

If the evil organization commanded in Europe its usual
army of spies and informers among cabdrivers, hotel
porters, shopkeepers and clerks of various kinds, it
wasn't surprising that they'd been able to easily locate a
six-foot-three-inch American with cold blue eyes and a
hawk face in a city the size of Liège. Bolan guessed the
inexperienced locals had been drafted after he'd wasted
the original hit team, because there hadn't been time to
call up top-notch replacements.

Okay, so the mission now resolved itself into a simple
equation.

Bolan's job was to backtrack Zulowski's flight from
Cologne to Luxembourg and find the medium he'd used
to make the holograms.

The Mob's job was to stop him.

In view of the intensity of the efforts they'd already
employed, it seemed to him there was only one way he
could make it.

He'd return to his hotel to get his weapons. Then he'd
go underground.

13

Going underground for Mack Bolan meant disappearing from the daily routine of life; it also meant anonymity and invisibility. It meant traveling at night in nondescript vehicles or in those where the driver was unaware that he carried a passenger. It meant riding the rails, stowing away and cross-country jaunts. At a personal level it meant that the Executioner had to stick to the shadows, togged in his formfitting combat blacksuit, complete with a customized harness that incorporated the quick-draw shoulder rig for the Beretta, a hip holster for a .44 Magnum Desert Eagle, two clips for plastic stun grenades and a watertight neoprene pouch for certain other tricks of his lethal trade.

He dropped from sight as quickly and effectively as a diver with lead-soled boots vanished beneath the surface of the sea.

In Liège the initial disappearance was the difficult part. The local Mob bosses might have been forced to call up an inexperienced snatch team after he had wasted their hit men in the Ardennes, but Bolan was certain there'd be backup units in place. The hotel would have been under surveillance, probably still was—there must have been a network of informers in place to have traced him there— there'd be spies at railroad stations, bus terminals, the airport. Maybe they'd even tailed the fake police car.

By now they would have been told that raid had been screwed up; the network would have been alerted. But he had to make it back to the hotel to collect his combat equipment, which meant that when he left the building, he'd first have to identify the shadows, and then shake them.

He could be in a tough situation if they pulled out all the stops. A professionally operated hit team working two-hour shifts was practically impossible to detect. You'd have a guy behind in radio contact with a woman ahead on the far side of the street, alerting a car cruising in a parallel street, which would be in touch with a cab driving in the opposite direction to drop a fare behind you, who would replace the first man. As well, a couple of standbys on foot could be called up to track the mark through stores, public buildings and apartment blocks, and at least one extra car would be on call.

Such high-powered tailing demanded at least twenty operatives ready to act, with two or three more as coordinators, working the radio terminals at some nearby base. It worked, in fact, on much the same principle as a radio-cab network....

Bolan donned the blacksuit, strapped on the harness and its accessories, hid the ensemble beneath a loose, lightweight sweater and a pair of baggy jeans and quit the hotel. His bag and the rest of his clothes he left in the room, with enough money to settle the account weighted down by an ashtray on the night table.

He broke a personally imposed rule and flagged down the first cab he saw crawling his way. "Residence Kennedy," he told the driver, naming the apartment block near the river bridge.

The cabbie nodded and spoke quietly into his radio. At the next intersection, before they turned into the park-

way, a second cab—this one with no passenger—
appeared from an alley and fell in behind them.

In the cathedral square, Bolan leaned forward. "I
changed my mind. You can let me out here." He thrust a
bill into the man's hand and walked hurriedly past the
steel-and-glass bank building to a department store on the
far side of the square. The cabbie and the driver of the
car behind were both speaking agitatedly into their
microphones.

Bolan raced through the crowded store, out into a
shopping promenade lined with ritzy dress shops and
then along a flagstoned walkway that led to a one-way
street.

His aim was simple: he wanted to tip off the surveillance team that he knew he was being tailed, and that he
was doing his best to shake them. He hoped they'd call
out all their reserves, so there'd be no extra backup
available when he made his play.

A line of taxis occupied the curb outside the opera
house. The warrior waited until the first two had been
taken and then hired the third, which had no radio, to
take him to the other side of the river.

He paid the cabbie off near the warehouse area where
he'd been before, and made his way to the street market.
He had no idea whether the team was still with him, but
he kept making the surreptitious checks that a professional would make to see if he was under observation—
sudden halts, changes in pace, a glance into an angled
shop window or the side mirror of a parked car.

If he did still have operatives shadowing him, it would
keep them hopping.

Keeping tabs on someone in a crowded city was no
problem, provided enough people were available. Without the mark knowing he was under surveillance, that is.

It was something else when an operative had to do the same thing across a barren moor, in a deserted village or on a long straight country road.

A stretch of water fell into the same category.

At the far end of a narrow space between two warehouses, Bolan saw a tug towing a string of barges on the river. They were heading upstream empty, toward Huy and Namur, perhaps to load a cargo from the Charleroi-Méziers coalfields.

Bolan glanced behind him, then sprinted down the alley. He tore off his sweater as he ran, stripped the jeans from his legs on the wharf beyond, then dived into the river and struck out for the barges with a powerful crawl.

There were six barges behind the tug. The warrior was treading water by the time the last drew level. He seized one of the old car tires strung along the side of the barge, and hanging on to this, he was dragged out of sight upstream toward the Kennedy Bridge.

To fool any pursuers who'd managed to stay with him that far, he didn't use the barge to ferry him way out of town. Instead, beyond the bridge, when the wharf he'd left was hidden behind a couple of moored sailboats, he let go of the tire and swam back underwater to the side of the river he'd just left.

He laid low until nightfall between two stacks of crated pineapples from the Ivory Coast, then stole a bicycle and rode eastward toward Germany. The warrior was underwater again when he crossed the border, swimming beneath the surface of a small river near Raeren, seven miles south of Aachen.

His target, thirty miles away, was a castle on the top of a hillside overlooking the Rhine. Schloss Königsberg, halfway between Cologne and Bonn, belonged to the new European Mafia boss, Vito Maccione.

Bolan scanned it from the upper branches of a tree on the far side of the river. The lightweight combat gear he'd packed didn't run to field glasses, but there was a DEP-350 scope mount on the alloy frame of his Desert Eagle... and one of the accessories carried in the neoprene pouch was a sight, modified for IR night vision.

Through this he could make out the general layout of the place. The castle was like a dozen others built on the high ground overlooking the Rhine—a complex of steep slate roofs, turrets and square towers topped with spired onion domes, wedged at several different levels into a cleft splitting the forested cliff.

The main entrance, Bolan guessed, would be on level ground, beyond the crest of the hill. On the river side, the property sloped all the way down to the road at the water's edge. The estate was surrounded by a high wall, and the warrior had no doubt there would be closed circuit monitors scanning every inch of the ground, supplemented by trip wires, sensors and possibly an electrified fence on the perimeter.

Even from inside, an intruder would find it hard to penetrate the castle. Some of the walls fell seventy or eighty feet sheer down into the faults cutting into the cliff.

There were also, the Executioner saw, teams of dogs patrolling the entire property with professional handlers.

If the Schloss Königsberg wasn't intruder-proof, at least from the riverside, it was as near as modern technology, unlimited funds and experienced personnel could make it.

Bolan was determined, nevertheless, to penetrate the defenses.

If he was to trace Zulowski's steps without a single lead, it seemed as good a plan as any to begin where the murdered agent had started: at the place where the stolen report was kept.

A building so heavily protected on the outside, the Executioner reckoned, might conceivably be less saturated with alarms within. The fact that Zulowski had gotten to the safe and had made his way out again unchallenged tended to support this.

Yeah, but how the hell had he gotten inside, in the first place?

Bolan was wondering whether he should cross the river, climb the hill and make a recon around the main entrance on the far side, when the castle—until then lit only by a few windows on one of the upper floors—was suddenly printed against the night with glaring brilliance.

Floods had been illuminated all around the baroque facades, and an even brighter light radiated skyward somewhere behind the towers and turrets, a white light punctuated at irregular intervals with pulses of red.

Bolan was staring in surprise at the unexpected display when he heard the noise, a droning clatter that overlaid a continuous whine approaching from the south.

A helipad had to be situated among those steeply inclined roofs, and a chopper was coming in to land.

He saw the navigation lights among the stars, then the dark blur of the bird's cabin before a searchlight lanced downward from beneath the nose.

The pilot hovered only briefly before he set the ship down, and it sank from sight onto the floodlit pad. In those few seconds Bolan saw that it was a medium-sized craft, no blister-and-formers skeleton but an executive-type helicopter capable of ferrying eight or ten passengers, with a full-length cabin and covered fuselage. It was a European model he'd never seen before.

The rotor whine and the clatter of the blades died away. Soon afterward the floods were killed and an extra row of windows lit up on one of the castle's lower stories. Maccione evidently had guests. As far as the warrior was concerned that meshed with his plans. Maybe a night of eavesdropping would provide him with a clue.

Because there was going to be one extra guest—uninvited—who Vito Maccione didn't know about.

The arrival of the chopper had given Bolan an idea. Off the highway, a short distance from the tree he was perched in, he remembered passing a brightly lit roadhouse with a campsite and trailer park. And among the trailers were pickups with specialized equipment that decided Bolan. The hell with any attempt to penetrate the castle defenses at ground level.

He'd go in like the other guests . . . at the top.

14

It was the gear on the pickups that gave the Executioner the idea that he might be able to penetrate Schloss Königsberg via the helipad that had to be located somewhere between the roofs and towers: lightweight metal spars with furled, brightly colored material wrapped around them. Hang gliders.

And if there was a hang gliding club in the area, there had to be a decent height not too far away from which the aviators took off....

Music and laughter spewed from the roadhouse, and most of the trailers were dark. It looked as if there were some kind of party going on. Bolan stole around to the parking lot and found, nailed to the trunk of a pine tree at the entrance, an illuminated board that carried a schematic map of the region. On each side of the Rhine, dotted lines, symbols and arrows indicated scenic routes, historic monuments, forest footpaths for nature lovers, and other tourist attractions.

Including takeoff and landing areas for hang gliders.

The area was marked as Königstein Schärfe—King's Stone Edge—and it was less than five miles away, on the same side of the river.

Bolan unzippered the neoprene pouch, took out a Swiss army knife, long-nose pliers and a tiny coil of wire. The smallest pickup in the lot was a miniature Honda. It took him less than four minutes to break into the vehicle, open the door, hot wire the engine and drive out of the trailer park and onto the highway. The music from the roadhouse was still loud and clear; nobody raised an alarm.

The takeoff site was a forest clearing that sloped down to the edge of a cliff. Below it, layers of trees dropped in the darkness toward the pale ribbon of the Rhine and the moving pinpoints of light that indicated traffic on the riverside highway.

A southerly breeze, which started at dusk, had freshened to a steady wind that would carry him effortlessly in the direction of the castle. Away to his right an approaching cloud bank reflected a yellow glare that must be the lights of Bonn.

The Honda was parked beneath the trees. He'd return it later to the trailer park, along with the sail... if he got the chance. If not, it would be discovered soon enough by other members of the club.

He unstrapped the glider and readied it for flight. Then securing his harness, he ran lightly down the grassy slope and allowed the thermal climbing the face of the escarpment to fill the sail and lift him up and over the edge.

The warrior turned away from the castle, wheeling into the wind with the cliff edge fifty feet away, checking out harness and lines as he gained height. The Desert Eagle, freed like the Beretta from its shrink-wrap waterproofing, hung heavy at his right hip. The wind numbed his face, drying the tears blown back across his cheekbones from the corners of his eyes.

When the street plan of Bonn glittered like the outline of a videogame on a TV screen, he banked the kite and turned back north, sailing toward his target two thousand feet above the river.

He was alone in a world of silence, with the lights of Cologne visible now beneath the stars in the clear northern sky.

For some time the location of Schloss Königsberg was hidden by the forest, but he finally got a fix on it from the illuminations around the roadhouse. Very faintly he could see starlight gleaming on the slates, a pale highlight on an onion dome. Then he lost it as the sail hit some turbulence.

Wheeling again, he broke the turn halfway to glide crosswind across the cliff edge and make time on the lee side. When he saw the castle again, lower down on his right, on the far side of the river, he sawed at the bar, pulling it back to gain speed and then dropping the nose as he veered once more into the wind and drifted downstream parallel with the Rhine.

He had to keep enough height to locate the helipad when he was nearer the castle, but stay low enough not to be forced to descend in spirals once he got there, which could alert guards in the grounds and make him a sitting duck once he was spotted.

Over unfamiliar terrain, it called for some tricky maneuvering.

For the third time, lower now than the lip of the escarpment, the hang glider swung east. Schloss Königsberg's turrets and spires were only a few degrees below Bolan's line of vision. Suddenly he saw the pad, a checkerboard square between slopes of roof above a grandiose pillared portico.

He put the nose down hard, swooping across the river in a long, shallow dive, and then swung back into the wind, the trailing edge fluttering as the plane neared stalling speed. When he was three hundred yards south of the schloss he turned through one hundred and eighty degrees, working the control bar beneath the A-frame to bring up the nose once more as he hit the thermal updraft streaming skyward past the terraced vineyards that lay beyond Maccione's property.

He was now approaching that property from the south, where the shape of the sail would be lost against the cloud bank blowing up from Bonn, instead of being silhouetted against the stars.

The forest treetops boiled up at him like the waves of some angry dark sea as he neared the Mafia stronghold. There was more turbulence here: the glider felt as if it really was a boat adrift on an ocean swell, lifted weightlessly and then dropped into troughs by the gusting wind.

Bolan planed down over the turrets and terminated the flight by turning one last time into the wind. As the jib of a sailboat putting about will flap, the glider's rear edge flapped when Bolan shoved the nose down and ran in over the checkered surface of the pad, spilling the rest of the air from the wing.

He halted two yards from the roof of the portico, rubber-soled combat boots noiseless on the surface. But had the fluttering of the wing given him away?

Before dismantling the craft he remained as static as one of the tall chimney stacks surrounding him, listening. He heard distant voices, a dog barking, the tick of cooling metal from the chopper parked on the far side of the pad. If the turbine was still hot, the pilot must have made a second trip since Bolan first saw the bird.

He laid the spars down on the concrete surface of the pad with infinite care.

A low wall separated one side of the square from the portico. Slate roofs slanted up from the other three, but a dormer projected onto the landing space from the center one, and this had been modified so that the original window was replaced by double doors of armored glass.

No stairway, no stepladder was visible; clearly the glass doors were the only way of getting into the castle—the only way that was legitimate. An alternative would be to scale one of the roofs, lower away on the far side of the ridgepole and hope to find an upper-story window that could be forced.

Bolan stared at the steeply sloping slates and shook his head.

No way.

He checked over his two guns, pulling back the nickel slide of the Desert Eagle to chamber one of the .44 Magnum rounds. He took one of the stun grenades from the neoprene pouch and clipped it to his belt. He removed a miniature penlight from the pouch. Then, warily, he approached the glass doors from one side.

When he was two yards away, he flicked on the light, angling the narrow beam toward the door frame. On the far side of the glass he saw a short passageway covered in dark blue wall-to-wall carpet, the outer door of a small elevator, the entrance to a stairway that circled the shaft. The doors themselves fitted snugly edge to edge, with no sign of a catch, handle or latch. No hinges were visible.

The Executioner frowned. Could they be remotely controlled from inside the building?

Uh-uh. Because there would have to be a bell, an intercom, a talk-through grille or a video scanner, and, after playing the flashlight beam all around the frame, there was none.

Sensors, alarms, magic-eye beams?

Zero.

Still frowning, he moved in until he was facing the doors...and froze, his right hand darting toward the holster on his hip.

The doors had opened, sliding soundlessly apart to vanish into slits cut in the dormer wall.

He saw it then, the small hooded projector hidden top center in the door frame itself. Cross the downward-angled ray and the circuit was broken: the doors were automatic, the kind used in any hotel, supermarket, apartment block or airport.

They also actuated a dim roof light that glowed above the elevator door.

Bolan glanced swiftly behind him. As far as he could see, the dormer would be invisible from any part of the grounds: the helipad would effectively block the view from that level. There was a possibility just the same that the opening doors would be signaled to security somewhere below. He stepped quickly inside, and the light was killed as the doors shut behind him. But now a red pilot light began to glow above an intercom at one side of the elevator.

The way Bolan read it, Maccione didn't need any sophisticated alarm system up there. There were no vent pipes, copings or ledges that could give access to the helipad. So there weren't going to be any chance callers there: the only way of making it was by chopper.

Passengers and crew, he supposed, announced themselves over the intercom once they were inside.

Since no chopper *had* arrived within the past few minutes, was there a chance that there was nobody listening at the other end of the intercom, that a pilot light there would have remained unnoticed?

In a Mob headquarters? The warrior wouldn't bet on it.

He'd better split before a voice behind that grille started to ask questions.

Unleathering the smaller, more maneuverable Beretta, Bolan passed the elevator and trod silently down the stairway that spiraled into the heart of the fortress.

15

Vito Maccione was thickset and muscular; he was shorter than Fraser Latta and much less suave. A scar from an old knife wound puckered the skin of his pockmarked face just below the left temple, and he wore his stiff gray hair in a modified crew cut.

The two men sat at the head of an ancient refectory table in the great hall of the schloss, a huge room whose ceiling yawned three stories above the floor, and which boasted a raftered roof and minstrels' gallery. Six other men lined the top end of the table and a pouting well-endowed blonde stood by a drinks cart in front of an enormous hooded stone fireplace. A burly guard was stationed in front of each of the hall's three entrance doors.

"Okay, so we fucked up all along the line," Maccione admitted hoarsely. "I don't want to hear any excuses."

"There *are* excuses, Vito," Latta soothed. "The reports tell—"

"Fuck the reports," Maccione snarled. "You know where you can stick them." He glared around the table, drumming thick fingers angrily on the polished oak. Precious stones glimmered from gold rings on four fingers on each hand, and he wore a diamond stickpin. "You, Giordano—" he stabbed a forefinger at the third man on his right "—you got an excuse for losing Bolan in Liège? With all the clout you got in that shitface town?''

Giordano was thin, bespectacled, with dark hair slicked over a narrow skull. Like the other five subordinates, he was dressed in a sober business suit, a telling contrast to the tan vicuña sported by Latta, and Maccione's ivory-colored shantung. Pursing his lawyer lips, he replied, ''Excuses, no. Explanation, yes. This guy is one super-professional. We had him sewn up, just the same... until he took that dive into the Meuse. Nobody could have foreseen that. We had a boat out in less than five minutes too, but he'd already let go of the barge that was towing him.''

''All you're saying is that you lost the bastard.''

''He wouldn't have been there to lose—'' the spectacles flashed at Latta ''—if he hadn't been picked up on a phony snatch. And then, if that wasn't enough, he was allowed to escape!''

''Now just a minute...'' Latta began.

''Or, after *we* had relocated by him,'' Giordano pursued hotly, ''if he hadn't been given a free pass by that third-rate team supplied by our dear friend from Cologne.'' He shot an angry glance at an overweight mobster sitting beside him.

''Shit, we had no time to organize anything better,'' the fat man shouted. ''After Bolan left the optical place and the Ardennes detail screwed up, we had to act fast or see—''

A tall bald man rose to his feet to interrupt, and then suddenly everyone was talking at once.

''Shut up!'' Maccione roared. ''Pack it in, all of you.''

He was on his feet, pounding the table with one fist. ''Get this straight. There have been fuck-ups all around. Number one, the security detail fucked up allowing this

Zulowski to make it to the safe and lift the goddamn report while I was away. Number two, the worst of all, Gallo's Luxembourg unit failed to catch him in time to stop the papers' being copied—and after that they allowed him to mail his damn holograms to the U.S." Maccione paused, his face flushed. He was breathing heavily.

"Just to keep the job nice and tidy," he grated, "Gallo then orders a sharpshooter to snuff the guy before they find out what he used to make this hologram, and where it is."

"Yeah," someone said. "Where *is* Gallo, for God's sake?"

"You won't be seeing him any more," Maccione replied grimly. "Guys who work for me don't make that kind of mistake twice."

He sat down and continued in a quieter tone. "Fuck-up number three, we snatch Bolan because we think he's in on the act and can give us information. Only he isn't and he can't. So what do we do?" The European capo leaned back in his chair. "We set the bastard free with a tip-off, like practically an invitation—" he shot a venomous glance at Latta "—to contact his bosses, find out what it's all about and start acting like a detective all over bloody Europe. That's what we do."

"You thought it was such a good idea, Vito, to create a special intelligence unit, feeding info to all the families over here," Latta said levelly. "Well, it was Schleyer's computerized intelligence that came up with the idea that it would be smart to kidnap Bolan and pump him on their communications setup. Okay, I coopted Rosi's boys in Washington to organize the abduction, but it was only because of Schleyer's intel."

Schleyer was another beefy man with cold, calculating eyes set unexpectedly in a prizefighter's face. "It seemed a fair deduction, given the trace on the guy that we had," he said sullenly.

"Deductions, ideas, traces!" Maccione yelled. "What I want is *facts*. I got two. This son of a bitch Bolan is still on the loose, and still searching, for starters. Second fact. The Washington snatch was the only operation that worked, the one piece of efficient action we've had since this whole goddamn thing started—and it had nothing to do with us. Every single thing *we* did blew up in our faces."

"Yeah, Vito, but look, man, the difficulties we had to—"

"You're bosses because you're supposed to *organize*..."

"If the fuckin' report hadn't been lifted in the first place..."

"What do you do if you get fed wrong intel?"

Mack Bolan smiled grimly. When the dogs began to fight among themselves, the prey sometimes was forgotten.

He was lying flat on his face, squinting between the wooden bars of the railing that surrounded the minstrels' gallery. The sound of raised voices had led him through the warren of passageways honeycombing the castle. Just before he eased open the upper-floor door to the gallery, he'd heard the elevator whine upward from some lower level. The opening of the helipad entrance *had* been signaled, he guessed, and someone had been sent up to check why no more visitors had arrived...and maybe why no second chopper was occupying the pad.

In that case, the glider would be found, they would know there were strangers in town and all hell would probably break loose.

That was a risk the Executioner had been prepared to take. He knew he'd most likely have to fight his way out of Maccione's headquarters. He knew, once he heard that elevator, that it was only a question of time before a guard alerted the Mafia boss. But he hoped—now that luck and good judgment had made him a party to a conference of the Mob's European chiefs—that he might get a lead in the few minutes that remained.

He'd learned so far that his own deductions about the kidnap operation that brought him unknowingly to Europe had been correct; he knew now that his other guesses concerning the hunt after him were on target, and it was interesting and useful to know there was a specialized intel unit at work, even if so far it hadn't scored too well. There had to be a first time for everything, and it was as well to be prepared.

The Mob had no idea what Zulowski had used to create his hologram, and they had no more idea than Bolan did as to what they were looking for.

During the next few minutes, Bolan sifted three more salient facts out of the arguments raging below. Zulowski had been chased into Luxembourg by a team under the orders of the tall, bald guy who was capo of the Brussels area, and the agent, at the time, was driving a Peugeot convertible rented in the Belgian capital, which hadn't been located anywhere near the agent's body.

The bald man, whose name was Campos, had discovered through contacts in the Luxembourg police that although Zulowski was on his way into the post office when he was shot, no letter, no package, no items of any kind that could have been destined for mailing, had been found on or near the body.

It wasn't much, but it was a beginning. And it was all the warrior was going to get, for the noise beneath the gallery had suddenly abated. One of the behemoths standing guard at the doors had softfooted to the head of the table and was whispering something into Maccione's ear.

"What!" the mobster roared. "Here in the castle? Jesus, what do I pay you assholes for? How can anyone possibly—" He broke off into silence as the man spoke again. Bolan couldn't hear the words, but he could see the darkening scowl on Maccione's face. "On the roof? Okay, send him in."

As the guard hurried to the door, Maccione stood. "We've got an intruder in the castle."

The hall echoed with cries of outrage and disbelief. "There *can't* be," Schleyer protested loudly. "We've got the best security money can buy, installed by the best technicians. *Nobody* could get past all the checks I devised!"

"Bolan could," Latta said. "He got out of my place, so he could have gotten into this one."

"Your systems weren't planned by my unit. If they had been—"

"Enough!" Maccione snapped, turning toward the door. An aging ex-pug, incongruously dressed as a houseman with a white jacket and gloves, shuffled across the floor. The man was shaking with fear. Bolan could only catch an occasional phrase of his stumbling, low-voiced explanation.

"...not my fault, boss...I saw the light, says to myself maybe more folks from the chopper—or, no, maybe another chopper. All at once I realize nobody came down, so I take the elevator... all in darkness, and then, right at the edge of the pad, I find—"

"You doddering old fool!" Maccione yelled. "Even someone as deaf as you would hear a helicopter putting down. And nobody's going to wait two *hours* before he decides to quit the first one! You should have sounded the goddamn alarm the minute you saw that warning light, the hell with waiting to see if the elevator came down." He shook his head. "Get out of my sight. I'll talk to you later."

As the trembling old man made his way to the door, Maccione took command. "You guys—" he pointed to the hardguys guarding the doors "—alert the whole team. Call up the outside men to surround the house, close. Assemble the soldiers on standby here. Move!"

He swung around to face the men at the table. "Giordano, Campos, Schleyer—take the second, third and fourth. I'll cover this one and the basement. Wallmann—" he pointed to the fat capo from Cologne "—you take a detail and flush out all the closets, service rooms, kitchens, passageways. We'll keep in radio contact. You know the drill. Latta can man the control room and liaise."

Shoes scraped against the wooden floor as the mobsters exited via the three doors. Maccione alone remained with the blonde and the two guards. One was a thin, wiry redhead with a foxy face, the other a blank-eyed professional killer with a lock of dark lank hair falling forward over his brow.

"You two stand guard in the central hallway," Maccione ordered. "Run, and I mean run, wherever the other guys call you. Bolan—if it is Bolan—will be alone. He flew in on one of those hang gliders and they don't carry passengers. So shoot fast when they corner him...and shoot first."

"You want this punk alive?" Foxy-face asked.

"Alive? Yeah. There are questions I want to ask. But cripple him good, okay?"

The men nodded and unleathered automatics from shoulder holsters—a Walther PPK for Foxy-face and a Smith & Wesson Model 59 autoloader for his companion. "We'll shoot real careful, Vito," the second man said, jerking his head to flip the lock of hair out of his eyes.

"Do that, Bruno. Lay off the balls, the kneecaps, the lungs. I don't want him screaming so loud he can't talk."

The gunners left the room. Maccione was alone with the blonde. "You better push that thing out of here, baby," he said, nodding at the cart, "and get lost awhile. I've got to check out the helipad."

"Vito," the girl whined, "do you have to get involved with this yourself? So you have a burglar. Can't the others handle it? You said we'd go into town tonight."

"This isn't any ordinary burglar. Stick around here and you're liable to get your butt shot off."

She pouted and wiggled her hips. "But Vito, I want to have some fun, see a show, go dance in a nightclub or something."

"I told you to beat it."

"But Vito, a gal has to—"

"Get the hell out of here," Maccione shouted, "before I get angry. You want some fun? I'll have you laid by every guy in the place, including the doorman, if you're not out of this room in three seconds!"

"My pleasure," the blonde spit venomously. "And don't think it wouldn't be, after what I'm used to!"

Turning her back on the capo, she walked out and slammed the door.

Maccione cursed and began climbing the stairs that led to the gallery. Bolan slipped away.

He wasn't going to learn anything more: the problem now was to leave Schloss Königsberg alive, and that was something he'd have to play off the top of his head. He had no idea how many of the enemy would be searching the castle, floor by floor. The gunners patrolling the grounds were being drawn tight around the outside walls. Indoors, apart from Maccione, Latta and the old houseman, there were the six mafiosi he'd seen around the table, the three guards who'd been manning the doors and an unspecified number of what the capo had called "soldiers on standby." Give it a margin of error: say around twenty.

He had seen the guns carried by Foxy-face and the cold-eyed killer; he was certain every one of the others would be as well armed. And they would be in constant touch, reporting back to Latta via the transceivers he'd seen clipped to the wall at regular intervals during his recon between the stairs that wound around the elevator shaft and the gallery above the great hall.

Getting out wasn't going to be the easiest job he ever tackled.

The glider would be out for a start: once it had been located, it would have been destroyed or at least immobilized.

The chopper?

It would be one hell of a long shot, even if he could make it to the pad unseen. The bird was a model he was unfamiliar with, and by the time he'd worked out the controls he could be dead in the pilot's seat.

Find some way to make it outside and scale the cliff then? Maybe, but right now the important thing was to check the layout, and at the same time, remain totally invisible.

He raced down the long hall outside the gallery door, which led to an open space beneath a dome painted with rustic scenes. Here another gallery circled the entrance lobby, with twin staircases curving down to the main doors and the portico beyond. Off this rotunda, corridors and minor stairways radiated in all directions.

Bolan heard footsteps, voices calling, the sounds of stealthy movement all around him. Half a dozen gunners, blue-chinned men with tight-waisted suits and blank expressions, hurried across the hallway below. They would be the soldiers on standby, ready to muster in the conference room. Bolan made it halfway around the gallery and dodged into a short passage curving away to his left. He passed two doors on either side, then came to another stairway.

Up or down?

Boards creaked above. A voice, quite close said, "Campos, reporting from second. Nothing so far. Checking backstairs and closets now." A click indicated that the Brussels chief replaced the transceiver on its wall mounting. Bolan saw feet, then legs at the top of the stairs.

He turned and went down.

A small foyer was at the foot of the stairs and presented four doors to the warrior, three of them ajar. Peering into each in turn, he saw a kitchen, bright with copper and stainless steel; a long narrow library furnished with leather armchairs, a pool table and books on glass-fronted shelves; and a small den full of electronic equipment.

Latta sat in the den, his back to the door, facing dials, switches and winking lights. A headset spanned his skull, and he was speaking into a microphone. As the Executioner glided past, he heard "Okay, Giordano, but you sweep the three floors in different directions. You don't want him to switch levels behind you, once you pass the halfway mark."

Bolan turned the handle and eased open the fourth door onto a flight of stone steps curving downward into darkness. A moist, slightly musty current of air blew through the gap.

Footsteps thumping on the stairway behind him prompted the warrior to cross the threshold and pull the door shut behind him.

His penlight revealed, at the foot of the stairway, a cellar with a vaulted ceiling supported on ancient stone pillars. His sweeping beam played upon broken chairs, tables, a tall piece of furniture shrouded in sheets. The cellar had no windows, but he discerned an arched opening that led to another flight of steps.

On his way from the elevator shaft to the gallery, he'd worked out the general layout of guest rooms, living quarters, the bathrooms. But he had no idea of the geography in the farther reaches of the castle. He guessed he must now be in the section built into the roof cleft. He went on down.

A second cellar was smaller and empty, festooned with spiderwebs and dust. An arrow window pierced the two-feet-thick outer wall. Bolan, squinting through the dirty pane, could see treetops far below, a pale ribbon of highway, the starlight gleam on water. The slit in the wall was too thin to take a man's head and shoulders.

A heavy oak door, spliced with rusted hinges, closed off an arch in back of the cellar. Warily he twisted the iron ring by the lock and tugged. The door opened about eighteen inches, first with a protesting squeak from the unoiled hinges, then with a screech that echoed loudly across the flagstoned floor. The warrior froze, the Desert Eagle filling his right hand.

Silence. He couldn't even hear footsteps or voices from the great sprawling mass of the castle above him.

Gingerly he eased his tall frame through the eighteen-inch gap, and encountered yet another flight of stone steps leading, in spirals this time, down into the darkness.

Was it possible that there could be an exit, somewhere down at the bottom of the rock cleft?

Bolan trod silently down fifty-two steps, circling within age-old stonework beaded now with moisture and hung with green slime. He could hear dripping water a long way below.

The stairway ended beneath another arch. Beyond this was a platform that projected from the wall of some kind of cavern, and whereas the cellar floors above had been flagged, this was carved from solid rock.

Bolan moved to the edge, the penlight illuminating slate walls that glistened with damp. Below the platform, the thin beam was lost in darkness, with the gurgle of running water now quite distinct.

He swung the light right and left, steadying it suddenly on another ledge, perhaps twenty feet below. Skeleton teeth grinned up at him, and beyond the polished curve of skull, he could make out a white cage of ribs.

Yeah, a way out all right—for those who had offended the ancient lords of the schloss. A permanent way.

The warrior turned and hurried back up the spiral staircase. He crossed the smaller cellar, passed the arrow window, and began climbing again. Half a dozen steps below the arch he paused, shrinking back against the wall.

The musty air blowing down from the upper cellar was overlaid by a heavier, pungent, more familiar odor.

Cigar smoke.

Someone was in that cellar, waiting for him to return.

He killed the light, lowering himself silently until he was facedown on the steps, then inched upward until his eyes were level with the flagstoned floor.

In the blackness ahead, he heard the tiniest creak of leather shoe, above it a whisper of indrawn breath. Twelve feet, maybe fifteen, to the right of the arch.

Bolan rested the elbow of his gun arm on one of the steps, his wrist supported on the ledge above. He stretched his left arm out sideways until his hand touched the far side of the arch, then he thumbed on the penlight and snatched his hand away.

The roar of the gunner's automatic was instinctive, almost involuntary. Stone chips and fragments of plastic erupted into the air as the penlight disappeared. Three shots followed one another so closely that the muzzle-flashes printed the gunman's outline against the wall in a continuous livid flicker.

Bolan wasn't aiming at the shadow; there was substance behind the flashes. He fired just above the flames, the Desert Eagle's gas operation and rotating bolt minimizing the climb and recoil after the first awesome blast. Two of the .44 Magnum rounds were enough. He heard the stumbling clatter as the hardguy was blown away before the echoes of that thunderclap double explosion died. The warrior was on his feet, racing for the next flight of stairs when the guy hit the flagstones.

He realized then that the footsteps behind him as he came down must have been those of the gunman, on his way to check out the cellar. He heard more, several more, as he burst into the small foyer. Latta was on his feet shouting, and appeared to be unarmed.

Bolan dodged into the kitchen. At the far end of the room there was a passage leading to a doorway. Through the glass panes he could see an iron ladder leading up to the graveled driveway in front of the portico. He ran for it.

Three men opened fire. Bolan somersaulted over a heavy wooden table as slugs shattered glass and clanged off copper pans hanging above a sophisticated electronic stove. He overturned the table, whipped out the Beretta and triggered a 3-round burst at the attackers.

One of the mobsters spun around, clutching at his right shoulder. He sat down hard on the floor, with blood spurting between his fingers. The other two drew back, and Bolan used the respite to leap to his feet and race for the door.

One of the outside guards, alerted by the shooting, jumped down from the ladder, a heavy-caliber revolver clutched in his hand. Bolan and the hood triggered rounds simultaneously. The glass pane between them shivered into a thousand pieces. A .45 boattail hummed between the Executioner's right arm and the black material covering his ribs. His own 9 mm fleshshredder cored the hardman's chest above the sternum. He was flung back against the wall, his white shirtfront crimsoned with froth bubbling from his slack gaping mouth.

Bolan reached for doorhandle, but a second killer waited at the top of the ladder, ready to leap to the ground. Bolan turned and ran the other way, racing up another staircase.

Shouted commands, overlaying the distorted tones of Latta's voice crackling through the transceivers, echoed from every floor. The target had been sighted; the hunters were closing in.

Bolan was still climbing when he heard Maccione's bellow from immediately above. He whirled around and quit the stairway at the floor below, racing toward the center of the castle.

The corridor was thickly carpeted. Fifteen feet ahead of him, a door opened and a man stepped silently out of a room with a long-barreled pistol in his hand—a beefy guy with a prizefighter's face: Schleyer, mastermind of the Mob's intelligence unit.

Right then, killing him was less important to Bolan than keeping his own exact position secret. He acted fast. Before Schleyer recovered from his surprise, the warrior launched himself through the air in a flying tackle, his head butting the German violently in the guts.

The breath exploded from the capo's lungs, and he staggered against the wall, trying to bring his gun up. But Bolan was already back on his feet and he hurled himself forward again, unleashing a karate kick at Schleyer's jaw, striking him viciously with the Desert Eagle barrel as he landed.

The underside of the barrel cracked against bone, paralyzing the Mafia man's forearm. His mouth opened, but he had no breath left to yell. The pistol dropped from his nerveless fingers to the carpet.

Bolan kicked it out of the way, holstered the .44 and launched himself at the capo like a tornado, his right slamming with piston force once, twice into the guy's solar plexus while the left, held flat and rigid as a plank, slammed against his windpipe. Schleyer subsided to the floor, gagging for air. Bolan left him there and ran.

He turned a corner, forked left, found another stairway and discovered that he was in the gallery surrounding the entrance hall. He wasn't alone.

Below him, six or seven gunners stood on the marble floor underneath a huge chandelier that hung level with the gallery railing. He recognized Giordano, Campos and the fat capo from Cologne among them. Two more killers—Foxy-face and one of the heavies who had been guarding the Great Hall—were climbing the curving staircases that rose from the foyer to the gallery.

It was time for a split-second decision. The Executioner reacted milliseconds before a deafening cannonade from half a dozen guns gouged plaster from the ceiling over his head.

He threw himself backward, opened a door, fell inside the small writing room beyond. Unclipping one of the stun grenades from his belt, he primed it then lobbed the plastic egg down into the hallway, slamming the door to the room shut.

Even behind the heavy door, the flat, ringing concussion hurt his ears.

Shaking his head, he jerked open the door and ran to the railing. Foxy-face and his companion were sprawled on the stairs; the other men were strewed across the marble floor.

But the gunplay followed by the explosion had alerted the rest of the mafiosi. Bolan heard Maccione's voice shouting commands, saw at the far end of a long corridor the blank-eyed killer with the lock of hair. The guy fired twice, aiming low. The warrior whipped out the Magnum, blasted off a single shot before he leaped up onto the railing.

There was no point going down the stairs. Foxy-face—shielded from the blast by the curve of the stairway—was already stirring and groaning. Bruno, the killer with the blank stare, was pounding down the hallway.

Bolan dived for the chandelier. It was star-shaped, hanging on a chain that dropped from the center of the dome, with curved iron brackets radiating out to support the lighted globes. His steely fingers wrapped around two of the brackets, the momentum of his leap carrying him in a Tarzan swing across the foyer toward the entrance doors.

Above the doors there was a pointed arch filled by a stained-glass window depicting some German hunting scene, with a ledge about twelve inches wide.

Bolan swung the chandelier in the direction of the ledge, reached it and shoved off the stonework with his feet, arced back toward the gallery and then forward again with increased impetus. This time as the chandelier stalled at the limit of its travel, he let go of the brackets to shoot up and onto the ledge.

The chandelier dropped back, and the unexpected, unaccustomed movement took its toll. At the top of the dome, weakened by the pendulum swing, age-old plaster cracked and fissured. Huge chunks broke away and plummeted to the floor. The boss from which the long chain was hung pulled free, and the entire wrought-iron fixture, weighing a quarter of a ton, crashed to the marble floor in a thunderous shower of brick dust and broken glass.

Bolan covered his face with his arms and burst through the stained-glass window onto the flat roof of the portico.

With the whole entrance facade of the castle plunged into darkness because of the ruptured chandelier cable, it took the warrior a moment to accustom his eyes to the night. Then gradually the sensitivity of his ears—conscious of shouts, cries, the patter of rubble inside, feet on gravel outside—was joined by that of the eyes. Outlines and then details assembled themselves: a mass of trees dark against the sky, a curving driveway, the glimmer of an ornamental pond, a stable block.

Hardguys poured into the castle beneath the portico, flooding into the ravaged foyer beyond, shooting questions. Somewhere inside, Maccione was screaming abuse at everyone in general.

Several luxury sedans were parked in the courtyard. Clearly not all the mafiosi had arrived by helicopter.

Immediately below the portico roof was a Mercedes 600 stretch limo, a uniformed chauffeur lounged indolently against a fender, unperturbed by the goings-on.

Bolan glanced behind him at the wall of the building and the helipad parapet above, cloaked in darkness.

Unsheathing the Beretta, his muscles tensed for the impact, the warrior stepped off the portico roof with its litter of colored glass. The drop was more than twenty feet, and although it jarred him from neck to heels, he was ready for it. The chauffeur and two gunners in the courtyard were not. Bolan dropped the man in uniform with a single shot as he came up in a combat crouch, firing two-handed. The guy choked and folded, hands clawing at his savaged chest. The mafiosi dived for cover and opened fire from behind the flimsy security of two large urns. But by then Bolan had jerked open the door of the limo and was behind the wheel. And the Mob preoccupation with security worked against them, for the Mercedes was equipped with bulletproof glass and steel body panels.

Slugs flattened against the bodywork or caromed off into the night as he turned the key to fire up the engine.

He wrenched the big car around and sped down the driveway between the trees.

It was nearly a mile to the gates. The wires must have been humming with orders, because the estate's dog handlers opened fire on the car with shotguns at several different points on the way. Bolan let them shoot: buckshot wasn't going to penetrate where .45-caliber slugs had been repulsed.

He arrived at the end of the drive unexpectedly. The graveled road turned sharply around a stand of birch trees and there, on the far side of an open area planted with vines and tomatoes, was a small, turreted gate house with latticed windows and ornamental iron gates between massive stone pillars.

Two men stood in front of the gates with submachine guns.

When Bolan drove straight at them they opened fire, muzzles flaming. Fragments of glass flew from the windshield and the hood quivered, but the limo didn't slacken speed. At the last moment one gunner dived away. The right fender caught the other man and tossed him aside as though he were a rag doll.

Bolan braked and nosed the bumper against the junction of the two gates. He downshifted into first and gunned the engine. The Mercedes pushed against the ironwork with all the power of its 300-horsepower six-liter engine. Tires spurted gravel; wheels spun; the engine screamed.

When he heard something metallic eventually give, the Executioner backed up fifty yards, then charged the gates with his foot holding the gas pedal flat against the floor.

The stretch limo hit the gates at around 40 mph with a rending crash. The bumper was rammed backward to crumple the fenders. The hood flew off and the radiator burst open in a fountain of broken headlight glass. But the two iron gates jumped apart and toppled sideways. And miraculously neither of the front wheels suffered a flat.

Bolan, who had ducked his head, sat upright and steered the damaged Mercedes out onto the highway. He didn't plan to keep the car long. The pursuit vehicles would be after him at any moment. And something under the limo's hood was screaming a shrill protest at the treatment it had received.

On the far side of the river he could see the lights of the trailer camp from which he'd stolen the hang glider. He knew there was a jetty and a boat yard on his side of the water.

The jetty was one of the many landing stages where tourists could board one of the glassed-in Rhine cruiser boats for river trips.

Bolan stopped the Mercedes two hundred yards short of the dock and killed the engine. There was a lightweight mohair sweater on one of the limo's rear seats, and he shrugged into it, covering the combat harness that contained his private armory, before he set off for the landing stage.

Arc lights bathed brilliant radiance onto the banners, the ticket booth and the wide, flat cruiser tied up at the dock.

Bolan bought a ticket, and by the time the three crew wagons pulled up behind the abandoned Mercedes, the warrior was pushing his way through the turnstile, on his way to a midnight wine-tasting trip downriver to Koblenz.

16

Only three of the car rental agencies in Brussels offered the convertible version of the Peugeot 205 GTi. Bolan hit pay dirt at the second. Zulowski had used his own name when he filled in the forms.

"It doesn't surprise me, Mr. Belasko, your checking out that one," the desk clerk said. Bolan was posing as an insurance investigator. "That vehicle has caused a lot of fuss."

"Fuss?"

"Why sure. The car was found abandoned at Betzdange, a small village in Luxembourg, with the windshield smashed and the gas tank full of bullet holes! You should of seen the director's face!"

"This Zulowski. Do you recall anything special about him?"

The clerk shrugged. "We get so many... he seemed kind of pressed, I remember that. In one hell of a hurry. And he paid cash." He shook his head. "The guy never even returned to reclaim his deposit, how do you like that! The damage would have been covered by insurance too. I thought that's what you'd be here about." Suddenly the man looked suspicious.

"Just assessing claims in general for an American affiliate," Bolan said. "Now this village—Betzdange— where is it exactly?"

"Between Ettelbruck and Mersch, on the main highway that leads to the city. But you won't come up with anything there. The driver who went to collect the wreck says nobody even saw the guy."

The clerk was right. Nothing of interest surfaced in Betzdange. The village's one policeman couldn't offer any help. No stranger had mailed a package from the local post office. Nobody had hired a taxi that afternoon to go to Luxembourg. Someone thought, just possibly, that they *might* have seen a man get out of the Peugeot and board a bus. But they couldn't be sure, and they couldn't remember what he looked like.

A check of the timetables showed that there was a service that would have deposited Zulowski in Luxembourg twenty minutes before the time of the shooting. And that was as far as the Executioner could get.

The inquiry came at the end of two days of painstaking and frustrating legwork, during which Bolan went over three times the route Zulowski would have taken from the car rental office outside Brussels airport to the village where he abandoned the vehicle.

He drew a blank at expressway toll booths, roadside diners, gas stations and taverns. Nobody remembered a particular Peugeot 205 GTi convertible on that day, or had noticed anyone who fit Zulowski's description. Nobody else had been around asking the same questions either, which seemed to confirm that the Mob knew where Zulowski had been. Presumably because they'd been chasing him.

That could also explain a slight time discrepancy. Bolan knew the time the Peugeot had left Brussels and the time it must have been abandoned in Betzdange. And they were too far apart—not much, but a little too far apart—for a guy in fear of his life driving like hell on the most direct route.

So what was the answer? The time lag wasn't enough to allow for a stopover and a visit to the post office in some town on the way. So it looked like Zulowski could have been making detours, trying to shake them off. Sighing, Bolan started varying the route.

And it was here that he hit the one positive lead in the whole investigation.

At a hamburger stand near Clervaux, in the Little Switzerland region of Luxembourg, he found a twelve-year-old boy who collected the license numbers of passing foreign cars.

And, sure, the kid remembered that day very well. He'd thought they were having a race, the small open Peugeot and the black Mercedes sedan—and although it was exciting, he'd figured it was pretty dangerous, broadsiding around corners on these twisty roads through the woods. He couldn't recall the people in the cars, but he did remember the plates. The convertible wasn't interesting: it was only from Brussels. But the Mercedes— he thought it was a 300 or maybe a 350—was not only from Italy, the registration was Palermo, Sicily, the first he'd ever seen.

Bolan handed the kid a ten-spot and headed for Luxembourg city, satisfied, finally, that he was getting somewhere. Palermo, cradle of the Mob worldwide. That was the clincher.

They'd picked up Zulowski near Brussels, chased him down into the Grand Duchy, hung in there however much he twisted and turned, and finally caught up with him near Ettelbruck, hosing his car with lead but losing him when he jumped the bus in Betzdange.

That hadn't stopped them from calling ahead and setting up the ambush across the street from the post office.

Why the post office?

Because they knew he was on his way to mail the second part of the hologram secret. And they had to stop him from sending it to the States at all costs.

Well, they had stopped him, all right, and whatever the medium was, it *hadn't* arrived in the States. But they hadn't got it into their hands, either. Bolan's own experiences proved that.

So, for the hundredth time, where the hell was it?

The latest intel narrowed the field.

Zulowski still had it when he left the wrecked Peugeot at Betzdange. There was no time for him to have stopped and hidden it someplace between the village and the capital. And even if he had, why would he have been going to the post office without it?

So, logically, he was carrying it when he made it up those post office steps. Yet nothing had been found on his body. And the Mob was still looking.

This mystery was beginning to appear unsolvable.

But there could be one other explanation. He did have time to stash the medium somewhere in Luxembourg city itself, in a place between the bus terminal and the post office.

In which case, knowing they were close behind him, he could have been on his way simply to send a message to Brognola, a cable telling where the medium was.

Whichever, it seemed crystal clear to Bolan that the answer must lie in that section of the Grand Duchy's capital.

It was about time that Mike Belasko, insurance investigator, made it to Luxembourg and started asking questions himself. . . .

17

Mack Bolan arrived in Luxembourg city after dark. The stores were closed, the central post office was closed and there was only a reduced night staff on duty at police headquarters. He checked into the Hotel Cravat, opposite the cathedral of Notre Dame, and paced out the route Zulowski would have taken from the bus terminal to the flight of steps where he was shot.

Luxembourg is built on a plateau one thousand feet above sea level. It is split through the center by the Clausen ravine, at the bottom of which the Alzette River loops through the capital, separating the old town from the new. Below his hotel, Bolan saw that the forty-five degree slopes of the Clausen were covered with floodlit lawns, dropping to an ornamental garden beside the river five hundred feet lower down. But on the far side of the cathedral, the walls of the canyon were almost perpendicular and the cliff faces were honeycombed with thousand-year-old caverns linked by passages hollowed from the rock.

Below them, steeply slanting roads zigzagged down to ancient buildings that bordered the river. The warrior stared at the descending panorama of stone facades and lamplighted roofs, of turrets and spires above the dark surface of the water. It could be the site of hundreds, thousands of dead-letter drops, secret niches or hiding

places where a man on the run could safely stash an envelope, a package, an apparently innocuous strip of
plastic or glass.

Bolan checked it out. The illuminated warren of medieval defense positions hewed from the rock was open
to the public. It would still have been open between the
time Zulowski got off the bus from Betzdange and the
moment he was murdered on the post office steps.

But there was no way Brognola's agent could have
made it to the caverns and hidden his package between
those two points in time; the detour was too long, there
was too much ground to be covered, even if he had run
all the way.

No, Bolan was convinced the answer lay somewhere
near the site of the killing and decided to confine his investigation to that area.

THE POLICE CAPTAIN wasn't overanxious to reopen the
case of a murdered foreigner—an apparently motiveless
killing—that had already been dumped in the Unsolved
file at the Commissariat archives. But the Interpol chief
whose signature had been forged on the Executioner's
letter of introduction was very important.

"Our files are at your disposal, Mr. Belasko," the
captain said, hoping that his men hadn't been too per-
functory in their inquiry. If only someone had said that
the damned American had been some kind of spook
from the CIA or whatever....

He picked up a folder from his desk and cleared his
throat. "The facts of the case, sir, are that the unfortu-
nate gentleman was shot down with a rifle by a marksman standing at a window on the sixth floor of an
unfinished apartment building. The structure is two

hundred meters away from the post office, directly across the street, and it was the evening rush hour."

"Nobody saw the killer . . . on the stairs, anywhere?"

The policeman shook his head. "Like I said, nobody lives yet in the building. The apartments are empty and the doors to the entrance are not yet being installed."

"So anyone could have gotten in or out unobserved. What about witnesses to the shooting, people who saw Zulowski fall?"

"There are many. Two ladies in the flower shop next to the apartment building, a man and his wife who operate the tobacco stand beside the steps and the newspaper vendor. Not to mention the girl who runs a necktie store, a match seller, passersby. Many people."

"Witnesses, I guess, to the fact that he was hit, fell down and died outside the post office."

"All but one. The man who sells matches is blind. He didn't of course actually *see* the assassination. But the man collapsed and fell in front of him, where he sits at the bottom of the steps."

"I meant that none of these people heard or saw the sniper fire."

"Aha!" The police captain was pleased. "But you're mistaken, sir! One witness did happen to be looking at the new building and observed the three puffs of smoke. He was confident enough, our killer, not even to use smokeless powder! Then, as the victim fell, the witness heard the noise of the shots. Otherwise we might still be looking for the place where the murderer stood. There are many tall buildings, and a dead man spins around as he falls, so there's no indication of where the shots came from."

"And your witness?" Bolan prompted.

"A lady. She was descending the steps as Zulowski ascended. That's how we know he was entering the post office and not leaving or just passing by."

"Did he have anything on him, such as a package? Would anyone have had an opportunity to approach the body and, well, take something away?"

"We think not."

"He was supposed to deliver a package. If it wasn't with him, I reckon he'd hidden it somewhere and was on his way to send a coded cable to his boss to tell him where it was. He must have known a killer was after him."

"Doubtless. But we found nothing on him, not even a passport. Certainly no diary or notebook or anything he could have used to encode a message. There was just a single business card with the address of his apartment here."

"Did you say apartment here in Luxembourg?"

"But yes." The policeman raised his eyebrows. "You didn't know? It seems the man's cover occupation for... whatever secret work he did... was as an accountant specializing in American company law. So he was frequently in Switzerland, Germany and Liechtenstein. But for some months his base has been here. The apartment remains sealed. Would you like to see it?"

"Naturally," Bolan replied, "I don't want to go over the same ground your men have so painstakingly covered. But, yes, purely so that I could get the feel—if you know what I mean—of Zulowski's life, I'd appreciate a half hour in there."

"Nothing," the captain told him, "could be more simple."

Ten minutes later, the Executioner left the police headquarters building armed with a list of the witnesses' names and addresses, the keys to Zulowski's apartment and a Xeroxed transcript of all the evidence taken during the murder inquiry.

He was crossing the roadway to his rented Volkswagen when the sound of tortured rubber registered in his ears. At the same time a blur of sudden movement on his right actuated the sixth-sense hair trigger alarm that years of self-preservation in combat had perfected. He hurled himself against the side of a delivery truck that had drawn up on the far side of the street, crashing off the steel panels to roll in the dust as a sedan roared past, missing him by inches.

Bolan stood and dusted himself off, refusing offers of help and descriptions of the killer car. As he pushed through the crowd of passersby who had witnessed the "accident" he saw the young woman. She was leaning against the hood of the car parked next to his own.

"You were right not to waste time with witnesses," she said quietly. "The plates would certainly have been phony, and there are hundreds of big American sedans in Luxembourg and Belgium."

The Executioner looked at her questioningly. "I guess I must have missed out somewhere along the line, but I don't think—"

"GSG-9," she said in a low voice. "From Wiesbaden. Second Surveillance Unit."

Bolan frowned. He knew that GSG-9—Grenzschutz-gruppe—was the counterterrorist arm of the West German BKA Federal Crime Office in Wiesbaden. He also knew it was now divided into four combat units, each thirty-six strong, and that the first two specialized in surveillance. He didn't know they recruited curvaceous blondes with flawless features.

"I can't ask you to come up with credentials in the street," he said. "Just the same . . ."

The blonde smiled. "Naturally, but maybe I can justify my interference—and at the same time convince you, Herr Belasko, of my bona fides—without an exchange of papers."

"Try me."

"Somebody tampers with the brakes of your car while you are consulting with Colonel Heller at the NATO optics laboratory near the border of my country. You have an accident and the car is wrecked, but you, fortunately, are not. After this I'm instructed to keep what my chief calls 'a benevolent watching brief' on you. Since then I have observed many things, such as a clumsy attempt to abduct you from the Silver Swan hotel in Liège by a team of bogus policemen. Your escape from this on the autobahn E-5 outside the city. A second attempt, which you evaded by diving into the River Meuse. A period of two days and two nights in which you vanish. Then a forty-eight hour span that you employ by visiting many places—and asking many questions—between this city and Liège."

"That proves you've been tailing me. Nothing more."

"You are currently staying at the Hotel Cravat, opposite the cathedral. Last night you retired early after eating at the hotel. This morning you visited Commissioner Wenzel and discussed the shooting of a Polish-American named René Zulowski."

Bolan grinned. "Okay. If you know already what my business was with the police, I guess you have to be official. But why are you watching me in the first place?"

"We weren't. You wrote yourself into the script unexpectedly," she replied. "The surveillance target was—and still is—Vito Maccione. And of course the undesirables he surrounds himself with. The Westphalian state government isn't happy to see the onetime leader of a foreign criminal conspiracy install himself between Bonn and Cologne. Accordingly federal help is requested and the BKA handed the job over to us. I was in Belgium, and only happened to run across you, because I followed one of Maccione's hit squads across the border.''

"And West Germany doesn't want neighboring countries pushed around by criminals based in its territory?''

"Right. The authorities aren't terribly happy either, to be honest, when gunfights occur in their own territory. As happened at the castle where Maccione lives. But doubtless you know nothing of that.''

"Doubtless,'' Bolan said dryly.

"My name is Alexandra Tauber. If you could give me some idea of what you are doing, and why, perhaps I could help you.''

Bolan gave her the expurgated version. "Zulowski, the guy who was shot outside the post office, had a package he was supposed to mail to the United States. A very important package. He was killed before he could, but he didn't have the package on him. He'd stashed it somewhere. My job is to find it and deliver it into the right hands.''

"And Maccione's people?''

"They want the package too. That's why he was killed. But they didn't find it, and they don't want me to find it.''

"So how can I help?''

"Right now,'' Bolan said, "you could come with me to an apartment Zulowski rented here in town, and see if we can locate any clues overlooked by the police—or the Mob for that matter, who must have searched the place by now.''

"Let's go.''

The neat, two-room apartment was on the tenth floor of a new building near the radio and television station. They drove past the huge gray building that housed the head office of the European Coal and Steel Federation and crossed the great single-arch Pont Adolphe that spanned the Clausen ravine one hundred and fifty feet above the river. Two policemen were deep in conversation outside the entrance to the radio station. As the blonde got out of her car, Bolan saw a nondescript man carrying a rain coat raise one eyebrow a fraction of an inch as he strolled past. Two youths lounging against an ornamental fountain in the lobby straightened up and moved away as Bolan pressed the button to call the elevator.

"The commissioner, I see, likes to make sure that his, uh, guests are well looked after... and don't run away with the keys."

"Naturally," Alexandra replied. "These are determined and ruthless people. They will undoubtedly try again. And since we have asked for the cooperation of the local police... well, however much they may admire our own efficiency, and yours, it has to be admitted that this is their home ground. I'm sure that Herr Wenzel feels simply that there may be angles unknown to us that he can cover just by being around."

Zulowski's bedroom was stocked with a selection of clothes a little on the staid side, a closet full of linen, drawers of socks, neckties, underwear, a stack of freshly laundered shirts on top of a signed photograph of a girl. The contents of the fridge announced his bachelor status: fruit juice for the morning, ice for drinks, end of story. The living room was a mass of paper: brochures, prospectuses, invoices, accounts sheets. Reams of notes concerning Zulowski's cover activities overflowed the desk, littered the bookshelves and tables, and even lay strewed over the top of a sophisticated stereo system.

"What are we looking for?" Alexandra asked.

He'd given the question some thought. It was useless to say simply a package: if there had been one, the police or the Mob would have taken it long before. But it would be equally stupid to refuse to say. Since the West German federal government would eventually be as concerned as Uncle Sam to squash the Mafia expansion plans in Europe, he saw no reason to hold out on the woman. He explained about the hologram medium without specifying exactly what it was that Zulowski had photographed.

But although they had a better idea than the Mafia thugs or the police regarding what they were looking for, they drew a total blank. The apartment yielded no half-silvered mirrors, no sheets of ground or frosted glass, no inserts of semitransparent plastic. After they'd spend more than an hour emptying and refilling drawers, closets and bookshelves, Bolan shook his head and walked to a window overlooking the entrance. A sallow-faced man with a lock of hair hanging over one eye was driving a Lancia convertible out into the street. "We're wasting our time," the warrior said. "There's nothing here the others would have missed. Every damned piece of glass in the place is a fixture. There's not even a portable shaving mirror."

"What about the photo of that girl?" Alexandra asked.

"It's all in the dossier the commissioner gave me. She's the daughter of a Frankfurt hotel keeper who he stayed with whenever he was in Germany. It seems they were... kind of close."

"She hasn't received any packages with a Luxembourg postmark recently?"

"The commissioner thought of that. And the answer's negative."

"What about other friends, business contacts?"

He shook his head. "Too complicated. No time. It has to be something simple. Hell, he had to use something nobody would specially notice, something that would be easy and quick to hide afterward, and equally easy to find again."

"You sure have the toughest end of the deal."

"Come again?"

"I mean the Mob has it easy. You have to locate the glass or whatever it is, recognize it for what it is, get it safely all the way back to the United States, then discover how it was used and repeat those conditions before you can really say you scored. All they have to do is destroy it."

"Guess you're right."

He relocked the apartment and they went out into the hallway. Apart from the back of a bulky man disappearing through the glass doors that led to the stairs, the floor was deserted. Alexandra pressed the button for the elevator and the grooved aluminum gates slid apart immediately.

Bolan stood aside to let the woman enter first, but paused. "Just a minute. That guy we saw—why would a man ride to the tenth floor in an elevator, walk out, then immediately take the stairs and go down again?"

"Because he was calling on someone else's wife on the ninth and didn't want to be seen going to that floor." She smiled. "Or maybe he meant to go to the ninth and pressed the wrong button."

"It would be easier to stay in the elevator car. It's not an express that passes some floors. We have time to check."

He leaned inside the car, pressed a button for one of the lower floors, and ducked out as the hydraulically operated bar slid the gates shut. The inner gates rumbled together, and they heard the whine of machinery as the car began to descend. The indicator arrow on the dial above the elevator sank from 10, past 9, to 8.

"Suspicious!" Alexandra chided. "That's what you are. Now we'll have to wait until—"

Something banged, twice, beyond the gates with enormous force. With an impact that appeared to shiver the whole story, a metallic thunderclap hammered the far side of the grooved aluminum. There was a subdued rushing noise, rising rapidly to a crescendo, from within the shaft. Gear wheels and pulleys, freed of their load, shrieked up the scale.

A splintering crash from far below echoed up the empty elevator well as the car, its twin steel hawsers sheared, plummeted one hundred and sixty feet to the winch housing at the bottom of the shaft.

18

After the steel hawsers had been sawed almost through, the police investigators told Bolan the following day, a particularly neat modification to the electrical part of the elevator mechanism had ensured that the remaining strands would part a few seconds after the car was operated in a downward direction.

"Okay, so we were followed to the building," Bolan said to Alexandra Tauber, "but they would have had to work damned quickly. Otherwise they could have killed the wrong people."

"They probably blocked the car on that floor," she reasoned, "leaving it until the last moment, when we were actually leaving, before they made that final electrical connection. But there had to have been at least two of them."

"Yeah." The warrior frowned, something that had been vaguely clamoring for attention beneath his consciousness finally emerging. Of course! The Lancia convertible he'd seen from the window: the driver, the sallow-faced character with a lock of hair over one eye. He was one of the mafiosi at Schloss Königsberg!

Bolan learned two more things before he left police headquarters. Forensic experts had now established that a third wound on Zulowski's body, discovered during the autopsy on his right shoulder, was of a different caliber

from the rifle bullets that killed him—a 9 mm slug probably fired from a submachine gun.

That stacked up with the idea that Zulowski had been
chased into Luxembourg by the Mob, and confirmed
Bolan's deductions concerning the bullet-riddled Peugeot convertible. But it didn't get him any farther in his
search for the hologram medium.

Fact number two—gleaned after Wenzel had permit-
ted him to put through a call to Brognola's office in
Washington—told him that a cable finally had surfaced
from the dead agent, but that it meant nothing to the Fed
or his assistants.

Bolan took down the text of the message, asked Frank
O'Reilly to put through another trace on the Stony Man
computers and hung up.

The cable, delayed because—for security reasons—it
had been routed through CIA stations in several different countries, read:

Shades of meaning: forwarding for lens treatment to
HB.

The message didn't tell Bolan anything either, except
that it had to refer to the package the agent had intended
to mail. "Forwarding to HB"—clearly Hal Brognola—
proved that. But the inference to be drawn from the first
phrase remained a mystery. And the lens, presumably
referring to the hologram medium, was as elusive as ever.

Bolan walked back to his hotel, ate a quick lunch and
crossed the street to the parking lot overlooking the ravine. Things were heating up—four sticks of dynamite
had been wired to the starter of his rented Volkswagen.

He dismantled the bomb, turned the car in at the rental
company's local office and took a bus to Grevenmacher,
a camping and boating holiday resort on the Moselle
River. Here, once he had satisfied himself that he had no

tail, he rented an '86 Buick Skylark sedan with tinted windows. Then he drove back to the city. He found a parking slot near the post office, fed coins into the meter and settled down to wait.

It was easy enough to finger the witnesses to Zulowski's death. The fat guy and his even fatter wife who ran the tobacco stand set in the outer wall of the post office. The blind match seller who sat all day on the sidewalk nearby. The uniformed war veteran who opened and closed the post office doors. A lean, lined newspaper vendor on the corner outside the flower shop. The curvy redhead with green eyes who owned the necktie boutique. The three waiters at the café next door.

Bolan's trained eye registered everything, but he was in no hurry to act. He wanted to submerge himself in the day-to-day activity, to soak up the feel of the neighborhood before he started asking questions. After everything had closed for the night, he walked back to his hotel and returned to the parked Buick by a roundabout route the following morning.

Twenty-four hours later he knew that the post office doorman got angry if the customers stayed too long after the place was supposed to close at noon, making him lose his usual lunch-hour corner seat at the café. He had noted the number of the Paris-registered Porsche in which a dark, smooth young man called for the boutique redhead every lunchtime and evening. He knew that the smart bespectacled ladies from the flower shop weren't doing very well because they ate their lunches from brown paper bags. He could tell which taxi it was that would call to take home the blind man, and which one had been ordered to help with the marketing by the fat wife of the guy who ran the tobacco stand.

For the tenth time, toward the end of that day, he checked over the Xeroxed statements made by the witnesses, measuring them against the flesh and blood human beings he could see.

Hearing a disturbance on the steps, the impatient porter had testified, *I went out and saw a small crowd at the bottom of the stairs. They were gathered around a tall man who had been coming into the post office and had fallen back so that his head was now on the sidewalk. He was clean shaven and his eyes were open. I could see that he was dead. There was plaster on the stairs and blood underneath the man.*

That figured with what Bolan knew of the doorman. An old soldier trained to observe. Crisp, factual comments. Eye for detail.

The wider of the flower shop women was returning a jug to the café. That would be Madame Grosch. He flipped pages and read her statement. *I heard my cousin cry out. I looked up. A tall man in dark glasses was lurching about on the post office steps. He sat down suddenly and fell back into the roadway. Then people rushed up and I couldn't see any more.*

A black Porsche drew up alongside the Buick. Seeing the dim bulk of someone behind the wheel through the tinted glass, the driver signaled—are you pulling out? When Bolan gestured NO, and shook his head, the guy scowled and shot away to double park outside the boutique. He leaned on his horn. The redhead came out, gesticulating. She pointed angrily at the clock on the post office wall, then at the shutters, which hadn't yet been closed over the boutique display windows. The Porsche accelerated away and shot a red light on the corner.

Her name, Bolan saw, was Estrellita Vatel. She'd been to the post office to register some mail before lunch on the day Zulowski was killed. *On the way out*, her statement continued, *I heard what I believed was a backfire. At first I thought maybe my friend's car was being temperamental again, but when I reached the steps there was a man lying there with people all around him. He was sort of staring at the sky. Somebody told me he was dead.*

The blind man of course had seen nothing. He heard somebody fall, heard another voice call for an ambulance, asked what was going on but had to wait some minutes before anyone could tell him.

Bolan read again the testimony of the person who'd seen it all on her way out of the post office, a Madame Sara Richter.

I noticed a man in sunglasses hurrying up the stairs toward me. I happened to glance over his head and saw three puffs of smoke, one after the other, float away from the window of an unfinished building down the road. The man gave a kind of cough and fell....

Bolan closed the folder containing the Xeroxed sheets. He'd been right. No doubt about it. There was a discrepancy.

He left the car and walked to the boutique. The redhead was a beauty. Her voice was deep and her skin, dark above the low neck of a white pique dress, positively glowed. Bolan pretended an interest in a display of silk neckties from Italy. "This one is kind of special, don't you think?" the girl suggested, sliding up to him. "The oyster-green color is definitely *you*."

"Perhaps." He fondled several others. "I had something a little more...sober...in mind. Maybe this striped—"

"Definitely not." She shook her head decisively. "I see you in a style that's discreet but *vibrant*. Those stripes are fine for northerners. I sold one to a Dutchman the other day. But for you . . ."

He seized the opportunity. "A Dutchman? Not the guy who was shot outside the post office across the road?"

"Was he Dutch? He didn't look it." She was indifferent.

"I'd have thought so, with that tall, rangy frame, pale hair and blue eyes."

"You got the wrong man, mister," she said. "He was certainly tall. But he was dark and his eyes were brown."

"That's not what I heard."

"But they were. I ran over there. I saw him. He was—"

"I don't see how you could tell," Bolan cut in, "since he was wearing sunglasses."

"He wasn't wearing glasses. I tell you I particularly noticed the color of his eyes. They had already begun to film over." She shivered and looked away, recalling the scene.

"Oh, well," Bolan said, shrugging. "It's not important. I guess I'll take the dark maroon one with the small white spots."

He went to buy some flowers.

The wider of the two ladies was convinced that Zulowski had indeed been wearing tinted spectacles, and her leaner cousin confirmed this.

By the time Bolan had bought a paper from the vendor across the street and heard that Zulowski had been behind sunglasses "as usual," the discrepancy had become glaring.

He climbed the steps to the post office, stood in line for one of the pay phones and made a single call. He asked Wenzel's assistant one question, waited for the answer then hung up and left.

Back in the Buick, he went over the Xeroxed statements and the results of his own questioning one more time.

He was clean shaven and his eyes were open.

A tall man in dark glasses was lurching about.

He was sort of staring at the sky.

A man in sunglasses hurrying up the stairs.

The redhead from the boutique had observed, correctly, that Zulowski had brown eyes. But the flower ladies and the newspaper seller testified that the eyes were hidden behind smoked spectacles. And Colonel Heller, the NATO laser specialist, had described the agent as a man "always wearing sunglasses."

If he *had* been wearing sunglasses when he was killed, witnesses would scarcely have noticed whether his eyes were open, what color they were, or that he was staring at the sky.

Wenzel's assistant had just told Bolan that the body of Zulowski, when it was brought into the morgue, was without any kind of glasses.

Yet no less than five witnesses had seen them.

He checked over the statements once more.

What stood out a mile, once you were looking for it, was that all the testimony citing sunglasses came from those literally in at the kill, witnesses who actually saw Zulowski shot down, whereas the folks who saw his eyes were those arriving on the scene after he was dead.

The conclusion was inescapable.

If the shades had been knocked off when he fell, they would have been picked up and taken to the mortuary with the body—and they weren't.

Some person or persons, therefore, must have removed Zulowski's sunglasses, taken them between the time he was hit and the arrival of the later witnesses.

What the warrior had to do now was find out who that was—and why he did it.

19

After the stores were closed and the area deserted, Bolan went over every inch of the ground. He climbed the stone staircase to the sixth floor of the unfinished apartment building and raced as quickly as he could back to the post office steps. He went from the steps to the flower shop, the café, the boutique and back again. He hurried up and down the steps with a stopwatch in his hand.

When he had finished, his original hunch was strengthened: geographically and timewise only one answer was possible.

The following morning he went to the tobacco stand and bought a pack of cigarettes he wasn't going to smoke. "And I'd like a couple of boxes of matches too," he said as he paid.

The fat man who ran the stand leaned forward across the counter. "If it's all the same to you, sir, you can buy them from the blind man on the sidewalk—there beside you, at the bottom of the post office steps."

Bolan raised inquiring eyebrows.

"It is unusual, I agree," the man apologized. "Especially as the sale of cigarettes and matches here remains, as it does in France, a government monopoly, available to the public only at licensed *tabacs*." His shoulders heaved in a Gallic shrug. "But what would you do? The poor man must earn a living. Officially, for the books, he is an employee of the stand. The local police are good fellows and they ignore the fact that he sits physically outside it.''

Bolan nodded and moved away. The match seller sat with his back against a stone column flanking the flight of stairs, his feet stretched out in front of him. A gray stubble covered his wizened face and his ruined eyes were hidden behind the circular black lenses of old-fashioned steel-rimmed spectacles. Below his tray, a crudely printed notice announced that he had lost his sight with the Allied armies in North Africa in 1942 and that he had no other means of support.

Politely, Bolan told the vendor that he needed some matches. The man cocked an ear in the direction that the stranger's voice came from, but he continued to look straight ahead, pointing to the tray.

Bolan picked two of the boxes from the tray and dropped coins into the man's seamed hand. As he turned to leave, he tripped clumsily against the lower steps and one of the boxes flew from his hand toward the blind man's face.

Instinctively, involuntarily, one of the peddler's own hands darted up protectively, was arrested in midflight, and then slowly lowered again to the tray.

Bolan recovered the box from the sidewalk and returned to the Buick. He'd found out what he needed to know.

At seven-thirty that evening, the match seller's customary cab called to take him home. Fifteen minutes later, it stopped outside a small cottage wedged between a bakery and a Laundromat in a suburb on the road to Thionville and Metz.

There was a pantomime of finding change, unloading the cardboard case containing the blind man's tray and stock of matches, and then the white stick tapped its way along a brick path and up to the cottage door. He fumbled for his key, twisted it in the lock and opened the door.

Once inside the musty-smelling hallway, he reached out one hand to check that the draperies were covering the window, then threw aside the stick, took off his dark glasses and switched on the light.

Mack Bolan was leaning his back against a door at the far end of the hall. The silenced Beretta in his right hand pointed straight at the match seller's heart.

The man gave a hoarse cry of alarm and his hand flew to his jacket pocket.

"I wouldn't if I were you," Bolan said quietly. "At this range I couldn't miss."

The wizened features twisted into a grimace of rage. "Who the hell are you?" the man protested furiously. "What right have you got to come bursting into a man's private—"

"Quiet!" Bolan interrupted. "I'm on to your little racket, so let's take it from there. I won't waste my breath telling you what I think of a man mean enough to fake blindness so that he can get away with a smalltime sneak thief act. It's a good scam, isn't it? Women leave their shopping baskets on the sidewalk while they feed coins into the stamp machine. They put their purses down while they check their mail, and who's going to suspect a poor blind man, even if they do register their loss almost at once?"

The cheap crook's face was contorted with rage. "Get out of here," he snarled. "Get out or I'll phone the police! I don't know who the hell you are, but I'll show you—"

Bolan strode across the hall, grasped the man's lapels, bunched his knuckles in the material and lifted him bodily from the floor. "No, *I'll* show *you*. But first I'd like to see what you're hiding in that pocket. Face that wall, legs spread, hands above your head."

He threw the guy away from him. As soon as the man adopted the classic frisking position, he ran expert hands over the skinny body, removing a small Allies automatic, minus butt plates, from the jacket pocket, and a Bowie knife sharpened to a deadly razor-sharp point from a sheath clipped to his belt.

The gun, only four inches long, could be concealed in the palm of a hand. Bolan tossed it, as well as the killing knife, into a corner. He jammed the muzzle of his Beretta into the match seller's spine. "All right," he rapped. "What have you done with the dead man's sunglasses?"

"What are you talking about?" the man whined. "I don't know what—"

"When he fell down those steps, his head came to rest just by you, didn't it? And in the general confusion you picked the glasses off the ground—or maybe you even snatched them from his nose, isn't that the way it was?"

"You're out of your skull! I tell you I don't know what you're talking about."

Bolan jerked the man away from the wall and hurled him into a cluttered parlor that led off the entrance hall. He crashed against a table that overturned and sprawled on the floor.

"All right, all right." The bluster changed to an abject snivel. "There's no need to make such a big production over a pair of fucking sunglasses, for Chrissake. Why do you have to get violent?"

"So you do have them."

"Yeah, if you must know, I have the bastard glasses. If it's so important to you. I don't see the harm in it. The stiff wasn't going to need them anymore. If I'd left them, the cops would've pinched them anyway. They were a good pair too. They would've looked great on me."

"Would have?"

"Sure. Would have," the guy mimicked, a malevolent gleam in his eye. "The stupid jerk must have caught them on something as he went down. One of the lenses is splintered to hell. They're no fucking use to anyone."

"Go and get them. And anything else you took from the body."

"There was nothing else."

Bolan hauled the guy to his feet. With his free hand he slapped the ratlike face once, twice, the blows sounding like pistol shots in the small room. The match seller yelled, glaring viciously at the warrior over black-rimmed nails as he felt his unshaven jaw.

"What else was there?"

"All *right*. There was a pocketbook. One of those zippered things. It was looped over his wrist, but it slipped off when he fell. The police would have—"

"I get the message. Naturally there was no money in it?"

"No, there wasn't. And nothing you can do will prove there was."

"Go get it. And the sunglasses."

"I tell you there wasn't any money. Not even one hundred francs."

"You might find it hard to swallow, but I'm not interested in the money—or the lack of it. So go get them. *Now!*"

Still holding the Beretta, he followed as the man sullenly walked through into a squalid bedroom. Beyond the bed, with its tumbled gray sheets, was a cheap veneer dressing table piled with watches, belts, neckties, billfolds, wallets, three or four women's purses, cameras, even a pair of binoculars.

He pulled open the top drawer and rummaged inside it. Eventually he fished out a zippered *pochette*, nearly new, and a pair of sunglasses with expensive tortoise-shell frames. The left-hand lens was, as the man had said, cracked, the smoked glass finely starred and splintered, though none of it had fallen out.

Bolan held out his hand and took them. Back in the parlor, he kicked the miniature automatic and the knife underneath a bureau. He slid the Beretta back into its quick-draw rig and opened the front door.

"That's all for now," he told the scowling match seller. "You can consider yourself lucky. But I'll fill in the police chief about your little racket, and I wouldn't like to find you back outside the post office if I happened to pass by tomorrow."

He went out and slammed the door, his hawklike features stamped with an expression of contempt.

In his room at the Hotel Cravat, he examined his prizes.

There was very little in the soft leather *pochette*. Any cash would have vanished within minutes of the theft, and the pickpocket would have plenty of black market contacts for the sale of driving license, ID papers, check book and credit cards. There was, however, a miniature diary, a small wad of folded wrapping paper, the end of a Scotch tape reel and a shallow cardboard box about six inches long. Inside it was a blank label with a gummed back.

And an unused cable form.

Bolan flicked over the pages of the tiny volume. Zulowski hadn't filled it in as a diary, a record of things done. He hadn't used it as a pint-sized engagement book. He had treated it as a mobile memo pad, full of entries in the kind of personal shorthand people often use. At random, the warrior leafed through and read:

RTB's ex AF...H'lamp bulb...Dks for W (NB no Scotch)...Check elec rpr + concge...B'day card for C.

The last entry, for the day he died, read: Send shades to HB.

Bolan caught his breath. Revelation. He recalled at once the text of the message he'd taken down from Frank O'Reilly, the delayed cable that had finally arrived on Brognola's desk.

Shades of meaning: forwarding for lens treatment to HB.

Shades again?

Of course! It hadn't meant anything then, but with what he knew now it was an easy read.

He picked up the damaged sunglasses—the shades—and laid them in the shallow cardboard box. They fitted exactly.

He nodded. Alpha plus for simplicity and ingenuity.

Zulowski had used his own sunglasses as the refracting medium when he set up his holograms.

No sweat now deciphering the scenario that final, fateful day.

Zulowski had already cabled a warning that he was going to send shades. And they would sure as hell be meaningful because, after the "lens treatment," they would transform the holograms into the Mafia report.

When he was killed, he was on his way to fill in that blank cable form to advise Brognola that the shades were on the way. After that he would have packed the sunglasses into the cardboard box, wrapped it in brown paper and mailed it, with the address filled in on the gummed label. Either from that post office or another.

It all figured. Except for the final entry in the miniature diary. An operative of Zulowski's experience didn't need a written reminder to send vital material back to his headquarters.

There was only one explanation. The phrase—the only one in the whole book with a clear meaning—was a deliberate tip-off. To Bolan or whoever might be delegated as a backup. It was a direct indication that the sunglasses were the medium used to make the holograms.

Zulowski was covering himself in case anything happened to him. And unfortunately for him the precaution turned out to have been necessary.

Bolan examined the shades, turning them over in his hand. He saw a pair of expensive spectacles with outsize lenses, one of which was cracked to hell. He hoped that both lenses had exactly the same curvature. Otherwise, if the guy happened to have used the one that got damaged when he was killed, then Brognola was right back where he started.

But that wasn't the Executioner's worry. As far as he was concerned, he had located the medium. All he had to do now was get it safely back to the States.

20

Two blocks behind Mack Bolan's hotel there was a picturesque cobbled square, one side of which was filled by adjoining five-story brick buildings crowned by peaked slate roofs and pepperpot spires. These were the royal palace and the Luxembourg National Assembly. In front of the Grand Duchess's home, which rose directly from the sidewalk, were two sentry boxes, each manned by a single soldier wearing an ornate uniform.

It had started to rain and the cobbles were slippery, polished bright by the light from the streetlamps. Bolan steered the Buick carefully across the sloping square: whatever happened, he was determined not to lose the Lancia convertible, but it wouldn't help if he allowed the sedan to skid on the treacherous surface and end up wrapped around one of the concrete posts in front of the palace.

He'd seen the convertible quite by chance, gazing out his window at the parking lot on the edge of the ravine. But it was the fact that Fraser Latta was easing himself into the car on the passenger side that prompted his spur-of-the-moment decision to give chase. He was down the stairs and behind the wheel of the Buick before the driver of the Lancia had maneuvered his way out of the crowded lot.

His plane didn't leave until ten o'clock the following morning, nor was there a Brussels-Washington connection until midday. Right now he reckoned he could afford the time to find out a little more about the Mob's European money man. It would be something he could give Alexandra and her GSG-9 associates to help them in the future.

The Lancia disappeared down a ramp that led to an underground parking lot beneath a modern apartment building a mile north of the palace. A few minutes later a row of lighted windows sprang to life behind a balcony spanning one side of the building. Bolan drove on for two hundred yards, found a curbside slot, parked the Buick and walked back.

The structure was seven stories high. The balcony with the lighted windows was on the fifth, overlooking a vacant lot that was clearly scheduled for development, as the area was littered with dump trucks, a bulldozer and a construction engineer's crane parked among the stacks of lumber and loads of bricks.

The apartment building too was obviously due for a face-lift. Scaffolding spined the edges of the flat roof and a painter's cradle hung at third-floor level.

Bolan skirted the concrete platforms where the foundations of the projected building had been laid down. The horizontal arm of the crane, higher than the roof of the block, was angled over the scaffolding. Halfway along, a cable supporting a bucket hung from the pulley that ran out to the end of the arm. The bucket was suspended just below the level of the building's third-floor balcony.

Bolan wanted at all costs to avoid entering the building at street level, either through the front or the rear entrance. For all he knew, the whole place could be a stronghold.

He looked up at the vertical, telescoped portion of the crane that supported the arm. It wasn't going to be all that easy, but he'd give it a shot. He began to climb.

The rain, gusting in from the west, made the latticed girder works slippery, and the higher he rose, the greasier the wet steel became. But the really tough part only started when he reached the horizontal arm.

The pulley, and the cable hanging below it, were about twenty-five feet away. Very slowly, the muscles of his shoulders and arms aching with effort, he started working his way hand over hand out along the arm.

Rain soaked his hair, ran down into his eyes and trickled between his neck and the collar of his sweater. The wind plucked at his pants. The farther he moved away from the base, the more the crane shivered each time he transferred his weight from one hand to the other.

His swaying body, hanging at the full stretch of his arms from the slender structure, was about eighty or ninety feet from the ground. His fingers were raw from grasping the squared edges of the girder by the time he finally made it to the pulley. He reached out one hand and grabbed the cable, hoping it might be a thick rope, but what he touched was a chill, rain-slicked steel hawser. He cursed. It was going to be hell lowering himself down that slippery metal strand. The wire was too stiff—and probably too smooth—to allow him to thread it around sole and instep and support most of his weight. His savaged fingers, thumbs and palms would have to do most of the work as he edged down.

He tested the hawser experimentally to check that it was securely braked by the operating mechanisms at the inner end of the arm and the foot of the base. Then gritting his teeth, he let go of the girder and transferred himself to the steel rope.

It seemed like a long time before his feet grounded in the iron bucket at the lower end of the line. He rested for two minutes while the heaving of his chest subsided and the throbbing in his hands abated somewhat. Then he shifted the upper half of his body strongly back and forth and began rocking the bucket in a widening arc, to and from the facade of the apartment building.

On the fifth swing, the bucket rose almost within reach of the painter's cradle hanging by the third-floor balcony. It was kind of ironic—Bolan thought grimly as the pendulum effect increased—that he was using the same technique now to get *into* Latta's property that he'd used to escape from his country place. And, more recently, from Maccione's castle.

Two arcs later he leaned over the edge of the bucket at the height of the upswing and seized the wooden railing at the edge of the cradle. The hawser shuddered and far above, the pulley squealed. Bolan felt as if his arms were being pulled from their sockets as his muscles took the strain, resisting the gravitational pull trying to swing the cast-iron bucket back down.

Panting, he tumbled forward into the cradle and let the bucket drop away. Thirty seconds later the creak of the oscillating hawser had died and the bucket hung motionless once more in the rain. Nobody seemed to have noticed anything.

Bolan hauled down on the counterbalanced rope to raise the cradle to fifth-floor level. He swung a leg over the stone balustrade, dropped silently to the tiled balcony floor and then padded toward the nearest lighted window.

He saw a deserted corridor with deep blue wall-to-wall carpet, cream walls and doors, and a number of sepia etchings in gold frames.

The next several windows were masked by draperies, but he heard the hum of voices from the brightly lighted room beyond the second. He leaned closely against it, but the window was tightly closed and double-glazed: it was impossible to make out individual words in the conversation.

He turned and stole back the other way. At the far end of the balcony he peered through a chink of a venetian blind into a modern kitchen. The window was locked, but next to it was a narrow, frosted-glass casement that was only latched. Bolan opened the longer blade of his Swiss army knife, inserted this into the crack and cautiously lifted the latch's metal tongue. He pushed open the window and squeezed through into a shelved pantry loaded with canned food, preserves and packaged cereals. Beyond this was the kitchen. He tiptoed through and found himself in a passage at right angles to the first.

The hallway was lined with three doors on each side. If his calculations were correct, the voices were behind the second on the left. He passed a carved ebony table with a Buffet oil painting of a harbor scene hanging above it, and bent forward to see if the door was old-fashioned enough to have a keyhole. It wasn't. The style of the place was luxury-modern, with satin-finish aluminum fixtures and sliding partitions that moved on rails.

Bolan had already recognized the suave tones of Fraser Latta, however, and there were at least two other men, one of whom was certainly the killer with the falling lock of hair.

He straightened up and laid his ear against the door by the hairline crack above the hinges.

"... view of the latest development," Latta was saying, "we think it reasonable for the moment to call off all attempts and plans to eliminate Bolan. Different units have been working at cross-purposes for far too long, but I have persuaded Vito that it's to our advantage from now on to play a waiting game."

"Call off the dogs? Is that it?" This was the killer.

"That *is* it, DaSilva. I leave you to give the necessary orders."

"Whatever you say."

"Why the change of plans?" The third voice was rough, grating. Bolan imagined one of the gunners from Schloss Königsberg. "For days we've been bustin' our asses trying to blow away this mother. Now all of a sudden you call us off. Where the hell does that leave—"

"The situation has changed, Bertorelli," an impatient female voice cut in. "Don't you see? Now that we have Bolan so well covered, why should we beat our brains out trying to locate...whatever the hell it is we're looking for? Now that we know he's hot on the trail, why not let him do all the work? Then, once he scores, we can destroy it, and him, in our own time."

Bolan realized that the dark, sultry, Katrina Holman must be in the room. The voice, talking emotionlessly of his own death, lost none of its sensuous charm.

"She's right," Latta said. "If we want him to act as our hound dog, we have to have him alive to do it."

"You said hot on the trail," Bertorelli growled. "How hot ... and what trail?"

"The guy with the white stick," DaSilva said. "Black Eyes the bogus beggar!" he sniggered. "Seems he lifted some stuff off Zulowski before the cops got to him."

"So?"

"So it's on the cards the prize might be among them."

"Then why don't we—"

"Bolan got there first," Latta said. "We're waiting to find out what he makes of his find."

"You say 'stuff.' So what did he get?"

"According to what I could beat out of the guy," DaSilva said, "nothing but a lot of crap. An empty cardboard box, a pocketbook, some diary, a pair of broken shades, shit like that. The creep couldn't even remember, it was such a load of junk."

"Maybe he'll remember later. Did he know what—"

"He didn't know from nothin'. He was just a cheap chiseler who got in the way and loused things up for everybody. Anyway he isn't going to be doing any more remembering. I did him a favor. His blindness is kind of permanent now." Once more the killer uttered a high-pitched giggle.

Outside the door, Bolan's flesh crawled at the cold-blooded, callous indifference to life and death that was characteristic of the Mob. The wretched little sneak thief had paid for his treachery and greed in spades.

"What we have to do next," Latta began.

Bolan froze, then jerked his head away from the door.

A key had rasped in a lock somewhere, a heavy door opened and closed. He heard men's voices behind him. Two, maybe three.

The entrance door was at the inner end of the passageway he'd crossed. He glanced back the way he'd come, the Beretta already in his hand. If he could slip through one of the doors opposite the room where Latta and his confederates were talking...?

No way. His eye fell on the deep pile of the blue carpet covering the hallway. His feet, muddy from the rain-sodden vacant lot beside the apartment block, had left unmistakable tracks that led from the kitchen to where he was now.

At any moment the newcomers would see them.

They would know wherever he went. But maybe not, if there were no tracks.

He whipped off the offending footwear, carried the combat boots in his left hand and tried the door opposite the one he'd been listening at. The aluminum catch slid back. He was in a bedroom heavy with the odor of expensive perfume. The flash of his new penlight revealed a bathroom that connected with the room at the corner of the two corridors.

He flitted through an atmosphere of colognes, steamy bath oils and scented soap, and opened another door. He was in an unlighted bedroom that smelled of cigar smoke. A thin slit of light shone from beneath the door; beyond it he heard the gravelly voice of Campos. "He *must* have it. He's booked on the Brussels flight tomorrow morning, with onward connections to New York and—"

The voice ceased abruptly. "What is it?" someone else demanded.

"Shit, would you look at that!" a third voice exclaimed. "There must be someone...*Hey! Latta! For Chrissake...!"*

Footsteps thumped toward the room where Latta was holding court.

They'd obviously seen the footmarks on the carpet. Bolan slid his feet back into the combat boots and advanced to the door. With luck he should be behind them now. He jerked open the door.

Bright light seared his eyes. Blinking, he saw in a lightning glance that Campos had opened the door to Latta's conference room. Foxy-face and Schleyer were standing just outside, the intelligence boss with a revolver in his hand, and alerted by the opening door, they were already turned his way.

He saw their mouths open in astonishment at the sight of his grimed and sodden figure, then he had triggered a single shot from the Beretta and hurled himself across at the passageway that led to the window overlooking the balcony.

They were fast. Overcoming the element of surprise, two of them had already opened fire before he was around the corner, the heavy slugs passing too close to his head for comfort and gouging small fountains of plaster from the wall.

Bolan fled down the corridor. He considered opening one of the cream doors, but discarded the idea because he might find himself in a broom closet or some other kind of no-exit situation, eventually opting to dive behind a heavy oak chest that stood beneath a window.

Shots rang out, a multiple cannonade whose power and ferocity battered the eardrums and set crystal pendants jangling on a pint-sized chandelier halfway down the hall. The flesh-shredding slugs buried themselves in the antique oak, scarred the cream walls, cracked the window above the Executioner. One of the etchings fell out of its frame and dropped to the floor in a welter of fragmented glass.

Ducked down behind the chest, Bolan took careful aim and shot out the central lamp illuminating the chandelier crystals. His end of the corridor was now cloaked in semidarkness while the gunmen at the intersection were exposed in silhouette each time they darted out from the connecting passage to try a shot.

Bolan held his fire and heard Latta shouting. Campos dashed past the opening on his way to the kitchen. He'd be heading for the balcony, probably together with

DaSilva at the other end of the apartment, to take the warrior from the rear.

The beefy shape of Schleyer appeared, to hose a spray of leaden death the Executioner's way. He stayed a fraction of a second too long. Lying prone, Bolan fired around the corner of the chest and drilled the intel boss with a 3-shot burst from the Beretta. Schleyer spun away, then dropped on his back with a thump that shook the floor, red blood bubbling from the holes in his belly.

The warrior took advantage of the consternation this caused. He leaped up onto the chest and, for the second time in less than a week, flung himself through a window to escape the murderous guns of the Mob. He landed in an explosion of broken glass, staggered, lurched upright and ran for the balcony balustrade.

Bruno DaSilva was at the far end of the balcony, outlined against the streetlighting thrown up from below. The long tube of a silenced automatic sprouted from his right hand. Campos threw open the kitchen window and jumped out onto the tiles.

Bolan whirled, choking out two single shots, one in each direction.

The maneuver was too hasty to rate a score on each side, but both men dropped, Campos thrown sideways by the impact of a bullet in the right shoulder. DaSilva fired as he fell, and although Bolan's shot flew wide, the killer's aim was deflected. Simultaneously with the *phut* of the silenced pistol, Bolan felt a red-hot needle thread his thigh...then he was over the balustrade and into the painter's cradle, lowering feverishly away.

DaSilva's head and shoulders appeared over the rim of the rail. Bolan fired once, smashing a shower of chips out of the stonework below him. But he needed both hands to manipulate the rope that was hoisting the cradle down. The ground still seemed a long way below.

DaSilva had ducked when the Executioner fired, but now he reappeared, pistol in hand. Farther along the balcony two more menacing shapes were visible. Latta, too, had to be outside the apartment by now. Bolan heard him shout, "Don't kill him, don't kill him! He might have found it. We have to know what it is!"

But DaSilva had already aimed his gun. Bolan didn't know how many times the guy fired—he was deliberately swaying the cradle from side to side as he lowered it—but he heard Latta yell again, "*No!* We have to take him alive."

The words were barely out of his mouth when a chance shot from the silenced gun struck one of the ropes supporting the cradle, shearing away most of the rope's strands.

The wooden scaffold jerked; Bolan played out the counterweight line faster still. Swinging wildly, the cradle shuddered downward. Then the Executioner's weight, seesawing it from side to side, took its toll. The last few strands of the supporting rope parted, and one end of the cradle fell away. Bolan lost his hold on the line, slid down the slanting wooden floor of the scaffold and plummeted twenty feet to the ground.

He landed sprawling on a heap of soft, wet, builder's sand. Glass from the burst window had slashed his forearms and bloodied his face; his palms were raw from the descent of the steel hawser; the flesh wound in his thigh was beginning to hurt like hell. But he was alive, on his feet . . . and running.

Over the pelting rain he heard Latta's voice far above. "All right, you guys, let him go. We can pick him up any time we want."

Bolan reckoned he might have something to say about that himself, however "well covered"—he remembered Katrina's words in the room upstairs—they figured they had him. But he filed the quote away for future analysis. Right now he had to get back to the hotel to dry off and clean up. He was already thirty minutes late for his date with Alexandra Tauber.

By the time he made it to the dinner-dance restaurant where they had agreed to meet, the champagne bottle on the table in front of her was half empty.

"You're limping!" she exclaimed, brushing aside his apologies. "Why did you have to put bandages on your face . . . and *why* are you wearing gloves?"

"I cut myself shaving."

"On your left *temple*?"

"I use the long stroke method. As for the gloves, we were always told at school that a gentleman—"

"And the limp?" She was giggling over her glass of champagne.

"It's useful if they play a samba," Bolan dead-panned.

21

Bolan came out of Alexandra's bathroom wrapped in a white terry cloth robe. It was three o'clock in the morning and they had danced—or at least stood upright and held each other on the dance floor—until the nightclub closed. She sat on the wide bed in a seal-sleek, dark red negligée that glowed beneath the pale glory of her hair.

"Shall I be your scarlet woman?" she asked, smiling. "Oh, but I forgot. You have to be *dead* after all that drama. You must want to sleep for at least twelve hours!"

"Alex," Bolan replied, "of all the things you could suggest, sleep scores the lowest rating in my book right now." He dropped the robe.

She eyed the lean, tanned, muscular hardness of his scarred body with approval. Fatigue and tension had etched furrows across his brow, but the contours of his rugged face were taut and alert. "Of all the things I could suggest," she said softly, "what would score the *highest* rating in your book, Herr Bolan?"

"I'll show you," the warrior said. He untied the belt of the negligée, slipped it from her shoulders and laid her down on the bed.

Curvy but slender when she was dressed, Alexandra's body was surprisingly voluptuous naked. The breasts were soft but well-shaped, the hips broad and firm, the subtle curve of the belly a delight to sculpt with the hands.

The Executioner felt the tiredness and tension lift from him and vanish as effortlessly as the bubbles from a glass of the champagne that was still in its frosted bucket on the night table.

Making love, Alexandra was warm and pliant and demanding, though her adventurousness never exceeded the limits of his desire. There was something nevertheless—a technique a little too practiced, a response almost *too* spontaneous in its small cries of joy—that posed a question in back, way back, of his conscious mind. Whatever, it was on a tide of shared rapture that they finally drifted into sleep.

At 9 a.m. they passed by the Hotel Cravat so that Bolan could check out. It was still raining, though blue sky showed through eastward toward the German border. Alexandra was wearing a white vinyl raincoat, white leather boots and a silk scarf tucked in at the neck that matched the color of her domed orange umbrella. She had promised to accompany Bolan to the airport and then return the rented Buick to the Luxembourg branch of the agency.

Bolan opened the sedan's trunk and tossed in his bag. "Careful," she warned, smiling. "If your precious piece of glass, or whatever it is, is in there..."

"It's safe enough," Bolan replied, slamming the lid. "Let's go. The rain will bring out all the jocks who usually walk to work, and the streets'll be busy."

The traffic *was* heavier than usual. He took the road that looped down beneath the huge rounded bastions of the fortifications to avoid the jam in the city center. They were crossing the bridge that spanned the Alzette River at the foot of the ravine when Alexandra said, "This little sneak thief you told me about yesterday—the match seller outside the post office—do you figure him for a member of the Maccione organization?''

Bolan shook his head. "No way. He was just a two-bit chiseler who happened unknowingly to have picked up something other people wanted." He downshifted and urged the Buick past a bus and a semitrailer that were spraying muddy water up from the wet road.

"But in that case," Alexandra protested, "why would he take your piece of glass or whatever it was from Zulowski's body? A pocketbook I can understand, a diary even, but a piece of... you never did get around to telling me just what it was that he used to make that hologram. What did you get from the bogus blind man yesterday?''

"Just that," Bolan said vaguely. "A piece of glass." The BKA and its GSG-9 affiliate would receive courtesy copies of the Mafia report from Brognola as soon as it was deciphered, but he saw no reason to divulge the hologram details at that particular point.

"You're making good time," the blonde observed. "You don't have to break the land speed record to get there!''

"Sorry." Bolan glanced through the streaming windshield and up at the cliffs, with their vast network of caverns, towering above them. "It's just that it bothers me to be stuck behind all these big vehicles on such narrow roads.''

Something was wrong. He'd been aware of it ever since he awoke—something niggling, scrabbling for attention at the margin of his consciousness. Something someone had said? A piece of the puzzle, at any rate, that wasn't right, that didn't quite fit. But the harder he tried to drag it into the light, the more elusive it became.

"Take the next left," Alexandra said.

"Are you sure? There's a sign up ahead with the airplane logo and an arrow, telling us to bear right."

"It's right for the airport, yes," the young woman said. "But we're not going to the airport. Take the left, then left again on Route 7 for Walferdange and Mersch."

He turned to stare at her. "What's the idea—" he began. Then it hit him, and he cursed himself for not seeing it before.

"What would score the *highest* rating in your book, Herr Bolan?" she'd asked him the night before.

But she shouldn't have known him as Bolan!

She had addressed him, correctly for a member of the BKA, as Belasko, when she introduced herself after his escape from the hit-and-run driver. He remembered her words: "Maybe I can convince you, Herr Belasko, of my bona fides..."

Well, she had convinced him all right, even if the bona fides were questionable. He'd been played for a sucker, but good. It was no wonder the mafiosi considered him "well covered"—with an operative actually sharing a bed with him, they couldn't have him better covered.

In the millisecond that all this flashed through his mind, it registered that she was holding a Browning-style automatic, probably a .38 caliber, in her right hand. And that it was pointing straight at his abdomen.

Involuntarily he braked hard, and they were both thrown forward as the car behind slewed across the wet road and blared an angry horn. "Don't do that again," Alexandra grated. "You might get hurt." The barrel of the pistol hadn't wavered.

"You made me break my sunglasses!" the Executioner reproached. He felt his chest where it had struck the steering wheel and drew a pair of smoked shades from his breast pocket. They had expensive tortoise-shell frames—and one of the lenses certainly was cracked.

"Put them back," she snapped. "You won't need them where you're going. And don't put a hand anywhere near your pockets again. I do know how to use this. Now, keep driving and follow the directions I gave you."

"So tell me, Alex, how does a beautiful young woman get hooked up with the Mob?"

"Don't worry about it." She shrugged. "We're both professionals. There has to be a winner and a loser, and although you played well, this time you lost. Period. Maybe it would have helped if I had showed you this before we started. It arrived at the hotel for you last night. The reception clerk gave it to me to pass on to you." She took a blue-and-white Western Union envelope from the pocket of her raincoat and eased out the contents with her left hand, unfolding it so that he could glance at the teletyped strips stuck on the cable form.

YOUR TRACE REVEALS NO ALEXANDRA TAUBER LISTED BKA PERSONNEL STOP GSG-9 ANTITERRORIST SPECIALISTS CONFIRM NO FEMALES RECRUITED SECOND UNIT STOP HB.

He drove for several miles in silence. They were heading north, roughly retracing in reverse the route Zulowski must have taken when the Mob were after him. They were approaching the small town of Walferdange when he said conversationally, "What's to prevent me from stopping the car in the main street here? Are you prepared to shoot me down in front of witnesses?"

"Use your mirror," she said. "The black Mercedes behind is Mr. Latta's. And before we make the village, a

Lancia will pull out ahead of you from a rest area. Bruno DaSilva will be driving. As a foreigner with no papers, do you think—"

"What do you mean, no papers?" One hand flew automatically to his breast pocket.

"Keep your hands on the wheel!" Alexandra's voice was suddenly hard. "The wallet in which you keep your ID is stuffed with newspaper. And in case you were thinking of trying anything when we stop, the ammunition in both your guns has been replaced with blanks. I was busy while you slept."

Bolan compressed his lips and said nothing. The rain had stopped, and sunshine was raising steam from the drying pavement as it curved between meadows of silvery green. A quarter of a mile ahead, the familiar Lancia convertible, now with its top raised, nosed out into the road from beneath a row of poplars and took up its station ahead of the Buick.

"As a foreigner with no papers, as I was saying, do you think any country policeman would believe you against the word of two carloads of Europeans, some of whom are local residents?"

"You tell me."

"Don't think, between us, that we couldn't dream up some convincing explanation...whatever story you told."

"Suppose, for starters, that you come across with a convincing explanation of where we're going. And why."

"Don't play dumb, Bolan. You know as well as I do. We're on our way to another of Maccione's properties. When we get there, you will tell us what it is that you took from this pickpocket and, if you have it with you, we'll destroy it. If not, we'll go get it, and then destroy it."

"And if I don't tell you?"

Alexandra laughed. She sounded genuinely amused. The coldness had gone from her voice. "Oh, but you will. Believe me, there are ways and means at Grindeldange. Some of Vito's friends are *very* inventive."

"Grindeldange?"

"It's a castle Maccione is restoring near Wiltz, overlooking the artificial lake at Esch-sur-Sûre. It's very picturesque."

"How nice!" Bolan said.

"You could feed a little more gas to the engine now. We still have almost twenty miles to cover."

Bolan's mind raced, wondering if he'd have an opportunity to overpower the woman before they reached their destination.

THERE ARE thirty-two castles listed in the brochure issued by Luxembourg's National Tourist Office—not a bad score for a country no more than five-sixths the size of the state of Rhode Island.

Most of them are located in the center of the Grand Duchy, north of the capital. Farther north, in the forested Ardennes region, there are curiously enough only four: Clervaux, Schuttbourg, Wiltz and Grindeldange.

The Mafia boss's most recent acquisition was a nineteenth-century Gothic monstrosity, with pointed-arch windows and a battlemented central tower. It had been built as a summer retreat by the owner of Europe's most famous travelling circus, and many carnie favorites of the period had been incorporated for the amusement of his guests—among them a maze, a hall of mirrors and a "tunnel of love" waterway channeled through the foundations from a stream that ran through the property.

The place had been uninhabited for years when Maccione's lawyers bought it. Much of the roof above the six hundred foot frontage had collapsed and fallen in; half of the fifty-two bedrooms lacked floorboards; windows were without glass and the stables had been gutted in a fire started by refugee squatters from Eastern Europe in the late forties.

The mechanism that drew the small craft through the tunnels had long ago vanished, along with the boats themselves and the hanging skeletons and other ghostly accessories supposed to thrill the lovers. But some of the designer's eccentricities, including the yew hedges of the maze and—astonishingly—the hall of mirrors, remained.

Mack Bolan's first view of the castle was limited. They had passed through Esch, a medieval fortress village clustered below a wooded bluff in a loop of the River Sûre. Two miles beyond the tunnel that carried the road beneath the ruins of the fortifications, the Lancia ahead of him turned in under an archway in the high wall of a gate house, steel grille gates swung open, and the convoy snaked along an overgrown driveway that ran through a plantation of pines. On the far side of the woods the enormous crumbling facade of the building was visible at the top of a slope of open ground that ran down to the shores of the lake.

At one time the slope had been a series of manicured lawns, but the grass was now waist-high, and wild tangles of briars submerged the balustrades and urns. Beside a derelict boat house, the planking of a jetty was rotted away.

The driveway curled around behind the huge bulk of the castle and stopped by a flight of steps leading to a wing that had recently been restored.

Bolan braked behind the Lancia; the Mercedes was close behind. DaSilva and the fat man from Cologne got out of the convertible. Flicking a glance at the rearview mirror, the warrior saw Giordano, Foxy-face and two gunners climbing from the Mercedes. "All right," Alexandra said, "you get out too, but keep your hands away from your sides if you want to live."

Obeying her command, he took in the possibilities in one quick survey. Four armed hoods behind; two in front, Fatso with a mini-Uzi submachine gun in his pudgy hands; the blonde with her Browning immediately in back of him; the blackened ruins of the burned stables twenty yards away; a stand of young trees on the banks of a stream fifty yards on the far side of the cars. No blueprint for a daring escape here.

Fraser Latta, his face split into a travesty of a welcoming smile, stood at the top of the steps. Katrina Holman, slim and dark in a jade green pants suit, stood beside him. Off to one side, glaring malevolently at the Executioner, Campos, the Brussels boss, nursed his shattered arm in a sling.

"Mr. Bolan!" Latta exclaimed smoothly. "How nice to have you with us once again! Let's hope that this time our hospitality won't bore you so much that you feel you have to leave."

"You know what you can do with your hospitality."

Latta ignored the interruption. "Alexandra, my dear," he continued, "we are indebted to you for so kindly bringing our friend here. And Bruno—" he turned toward DaSilva "—it was good of you to lead the way. To spare him the tedious preliminaries to the entertainment we have prepared, perhaps you would be kind enough to make Mr. Bolan comfortable for the time being, eh?''

Too late, the warrior swung around. He saw the grin on the face of one of the gunners, and he was aware of movement to his right. Then the butt of DaSilva's Smith & Wesson landed behind his ear and the sky went dark.

22

Bolan winced at the sledgehammer blows raining on the inside of his skull. The blows became stronger and stronger, reverberating painfully, until at last the hammerhead burst its way through at a weak point and daylight came flooding in.

The warrior blinked his eyes. It wasn't daylight at all, he saw, but the illumination of an unshaded electric bulb hanging ten feet above his head.

He was lying on his back on the floor, naked. He could feel the cool, gritty surface of concrete against his calves, his haunches, his shoulder blades. He was also—he flexed his muscles—scientifically bound, spread-eagled to four rings set in the concrete. If he twisted his head he could see the iron circlets and the wire biting into his flesh.

As far as he could, he took in the room. It was a cellar, about twenty feet square, with no skylight or windows. It was empty except for an apparatus that looked like part of a stereo system, and another that was basically a tubular steel tripod with a T-shaped crosspiece and a length of rubber tubing leading to it.

Bolan tested his bonds with wrists and fingers. Escape was a no-go situation. He was attached to the rings with chicken wire, which had been fastened by an expert.

Struggling would only chafe away the flesh from his wrists and ankles, and he was already uncomfortable enough, stretched out to the full extent of his legs and arms. His palms and the insides of his fingers were still raw from his exploits on the crane the previous night.

"Damn!" he said between set teeth.

There was a deep chuckle from the dead area behind his head. "Welcome back to today, Mr. Bolan!" Fraser Latta's voice intoned.

Bolan twisted his head until eventually he was able to see the tall, bulky figure of the Mafia's European laundryman seated comfortably on a chair tipped against the wall.

"It seems you have me at a disadvantage."

"And I intend to keep you there," Latta replied genially. "I had only intended to question you in general terms when you were my guest before. But we know a great deal more now, and so do you. The questions must therefore be specific. So, you will tell me exactly what it was that the tiresome Zulowski used to make his holograms. Your bag has been searched and you do not appear to have it with you. You will therefore tell me also where you have hidden it so that it can be destroyed. And then the hologram will remain forever useless, and we can carry on with the work you have interrupted."

"After destroying me too?"

"That depends on your cooperation. Certainly we shall take steps to ensure that you will be, in certain ways, useless. Deprived of the gift of sight for instance. Or confined to a wheelchair. Alive maybe, but unable to hinder us any further."

"Your argument is based on a false premise," Bolan said.

"Really? I'd be interested to hear what."

"You assume I'll answer your questions."

Latta laughed again. "Oh, come now! You know as well as I do that anyone, anyone at all, can be broken. Eventually. It's no more than a question of time, and we have plenty of that. Let me explain the method we'll use."

He rose and walked slowly around the warrior to the two pieces of apparatus on the cellar floor. "An item," he said, touching the tripod, "of homely garden equipment. I'm sure you've seen one before. Through the rubber tube, water flows under pressure into the crosspiece, revolving it about its central axis, which is balanced on delicate bearings. At the same time, as it swings around, the water emerges from small holes along its length in the form of a fine spray. Since the water pressure can be varied, the speed of the crosspiece—and thus the distance and the course traced by the spray—are in effect random. A tripod properly set up can water a fair section of garden very thoroughly in quite a short time.

"That, of course, is of no more than academic interest," he continued as he moved across to the second piece of equipment and stood with one hand resting on it, looking down at Bolan. "But with this we come into the realm of practical applications. It is in fact an electrical generator . . . and water is a perfect conductor."

A draft drifting past Bolan's naked trussed body strengthened. He heard footsteps, and tall white boots creaked into his field of vision. It was Alexandra, still wearing her vinyl raincoat.

"Very nice," she said, staring down at him, "although I prefer you in a more . . . active . . . position."

"He'll be active enough when our experiment starts," Latta told her. "Perhaps, my dear, you would like to explain?"

"It's very simple," Alexandra said. "As you heard, water is a perfect conductor. So if we connect the generator output, which is variable, to the crosspiece, the water droplets as they spray out and spiral around will carry the charge, as long as there is continuous contact, drop by drop, back to the metal of the crosspiece. Anyone on whom the spray falls when this contact exists will therefore receive a shock—unless or until the particles of water separate, when the circuit is broken."

She walked across to the tripod and spun the crosspiece. It revolved smoothly and silently on its bearings. She added, "Since the speed, and therefore the exact direction, of the spray is indeterminate—as is the frequency of the electric current it carries—the amount of time a person under the spray would in fact receive electric shocks is also totally random."

"The point of all this," Latta explained, "is that in most forms of, uh, persuasion, the person to be persuaded can see the hot iron or the needle or the whip or the hand on the electrical switch and can therefore in some way tense himself, employ his Zen techniques or tighten up in anticipation of the pain. Can begin, even, to combat it. But imagine, as I am sure a man in your position easily could, the victim in the dark awaiting the arbitrary movements of a spray like this, knowing that even when the water reaches him, it might not carry a charge. And that the charge itself, and thus the amount of pain it produces, is also variable. Infinitely, Mr. Bolan."

"You might think it unduly complex," Alexandra continued, "but the system has been perfected to save time. Yours as well as ours. The disintegration of self-control actually does arrive much more quickly. It's like the ancient Chinese dripping tap torture, with uncertainty thrown in to add a ... well, psychological element."

"Labor saving," Latta added. "And of course, as the floor becomes covered with a thin overall layer of moisture, a charge carried by the spray that falls short of the body can still be transmitted to it. If you think, you'll see that this is why we use iron rings and steel wire to secure you. Both are admirable conductors."

"If you spent less time on melodrama and more on organization," Bolan said, "your plans might be a little more successful."

"We'll see how successful we are very shortly," Latta said. He moved to a faucet from which the rubber tube feeding the sprinkler ran and turned the brass wheel, opening the faucet.

For a moment nothing happened, then, with a sudden hiss, the crosspiece jerked into motion. From each end, a fan of spray feathered out, describing a moving spiral of mist in the air. As the speed of the sprinkler increased, the two fans coalesced to form a single arc scything this way and that across the brightly lighted cellar.

Bolan saw the figure eight patterns the moisture made on the dusty floor. Then a trailing end of the spray fell once, twice and—after a slight delay—a third time coldly over the goose bumps on his skin. By the time he caught his breath, the entire floor was shining, uniformly wet.

Alexandra Tauber was attaching some piece of equipment to the faucet. "This," Latta said, raising his voice over the swishing of the sprinkler, "automatically varies the water pressure revolving the crosspiece, so the pattern of the spray will vary also. You may watch for a few minutes before we leave you and cut the light. But first let me show you the best part." He wheeled the generator closer to the tripod and drew on rubber gloves. Swiftly he made a connection.

The water was falling sporadically across the Executioner's flesh, sometimes in a fine veil, sometimes with a certain force. But now, suddenly, one time, the unmistakable tingle of mild shock whipped across his belly and up over his shoulder to his right arm.

Latta was operating a rheostat control of the generator. Again water swept over the warrior—and a hoarse cry burst from Bolan's lips as something that felt like a red-hot whip scalded the bullet wound in his thigh. A violent spasm arched his body up from the iron rings. Seconds later a tongue of flame licked at his belly, and his chest was savaged. Bolan couldn't hold back a scream.

Alexandra Tauber's pale plastic raincoat was shiny with water. Water dropped from the ceiling, washed across the floor and streamed down the cellar walls to gurgle into a drain. The warrior felt it clammy against his back as the pain in his tortured body subsided. But there was no more water in the air. Latta had switched the apparatus off.

He spoke, his suit dark with moisture, from the far side of the room. "We'll leave you now. There are dual controls outside this cellar. At indeterminate times in the hours that follow, the sprinkler will be turned on—and off—sometimes with an electrical charge, sometimes not. You have already had a taste both of the mild and the fairly strong current. Although it can of course be stronger still if we wish. Now—" he walked to the door "—we don't wish to keep on interrupting you with tedious requests as to whether you are ready to talk. So every sound you make will be taped, and at intervals we'll play back the tapes. When we judge from the noises that you, uh, have something to say, we'll return. But not before."

He ushered the young woman out, switched off the light and slammed the door.

In the sudden intense darkness Bolan lay wondering what the hell he could do. There was nothing.

His bonds were unbreakable; since he was naked there was nothing he could reach or hope to adapt from his clothes.

The secret of the hologram was safe. He'd diverted attention from Zulowski's shades by simply stuffing them into his breast pocket, and the explanation of why a man would carry sunglasses with one lens broken was taken care of by the fact that he had allowed himself to be thrown forward against the wheel under heavy braking when Alexandra revealed her true colors.

But how in hell was he going to get those shades out of this crumbling castle? How was he to escape from the cellar?

The thought that he might crack and spill the secret never occurred to him. Bolan had stood up under torture before. He had no psychiatric conditioning, no posthypnotic implants in his mind. The combined onslaughts of pain coupled with uncertainty might break him, as Alexandra had suggested, into a gibbering wreck. He might be unable to stop himself screaming. But he would never crack; he would will himself to die before he told the Mafia what they wanted—needed—to know.

The future of too many ordinary men and women depended on his determination for him to think otherwise.

Stretched there as humiliatingly as a specimen on a microscope slide, the flesh tensed for the cold caress of a spray that might or might not come, the agony that might—or might not—come with it, he summoned the totality of his iron will to combat the hours of anguish to come.

Water hissed suddenly into action as the sprinkler jingled into motion. A wedge of light opened into the dark and then vanished as the cellar door opened and closed. In the instant of illumination he saw again the white vinyl raincoat. Cold mist trailed over his legs. He tensed, but there was no shock, mild or violent, this time. The water swept across him again.

He could hear the rustle of the vinyl by the generator. A pencil of light from a pocket flashlight lanced the blackness. Footsteps splashed across the cellar floor and stopped somewhere behind him. Again and again the spray washed over his body, but there was still no shock.

Water splatted against the vinyl. The girl was on one knee by the iron ring to which his right hand was wired. When he craned his head over his shoulder he saw the torchlight sliding over the contours of the polished material sheathing her body.

An instant later there was a sharp snick and his hand was free.

"What's going on?"

"Shh!" The whisper was urgent. "Don't forget the tape! And you're supposed to be on the wrong end of a series of electric shocks, so it would help if you could groan from time to time."

He uttered a hoarse cry. His left hand was free. The light beam stabbed down toward his feet. Again she crouched, a strange figure shining wetly in the diffuse light. Then he was completely free, sitting up on the cold floor trying to massage life back into his limbs.

Three minutes later the door opened and he was pushed out of the cellar into a flagstone passageway. Duplicate controls for the sprinkler and generator were set into an electrical console screwed to the wall. The door shut, killing the swish of water. He turned . . . and saw in the harsh light of an overhead bulb that his rescuer wasn't Alexandra, but Katrina Holman.

"We should be all right for at least ten minutes," she murmured. "I'm supposed to be assigned to the first shift at the controls. Even if they did listen to the tape so early, they'd just think I'd deliberately left a gap in the 'treatment.' They'll be expecting that anyway."

"I don't want to seem ungrateful," Bolan said, "but could you tell me what the hell's going on?"

Katrina smiled. "You're not going to believe this," she said, "but I work with the BKA federal police headquarters in Wiesbaden."

He stared. "Don't tell me. The second unit of GSG-9?"

The young woman in the raincoat shook her head. "Uh-uh. As you know, they don't employ women. I'm with the surveillance section of TE-2."

"Okay." That figured. He knew that TE-2 signified the control intelligence unit of the BKA's antiterrorist and anticonspiracy division. And they *would* use women.

"Alexandra, being a phony, has no idea that I'm the genuine article, of course," Katrina said. "But we have been watching her, and the Maccione-Latta setup, for months. I was put in to keep tabs on Latta when he took a shine to me at some industrialists' shindig.

"I'm sorry." She was all contrition. "You must be frozen! Your clothes are in this closet. Here, put them on quickly." She took out the garments and handed them to him one by one. He patted the breast pocket of the jacket. The shades—the vital link in the chain that would strangle the Mob's plans for Europe—were still there. He stifled a sigh of relief but said nothing. It was just possible that the whole rescue deal was another double bluff, that Katrina, too, really was working for Latta, that they hoped in the psychological release of his supposed rescue he would confide in her what he refused to reveal under torture. Latta was a man whose mind was that subtle.

In any event she'd have to provide more positive proof of her trustworthiness before he came across himself with the truth, the whole truth, and nothing but the truth.

While he dressed, she shrugged out of the vinyl raincoat and hung it up in the closet. "In case Alexandra misses it," she explained. "But we have very little time. Within the next ten minutes Latta's going to realize from the tape that you're no longer in the cellar, and that will tip them off that I have to be responsible."

He nodded. "And they won't wait to ask questions, will they?"

"Right. My car is out front. If we can make it to that before they catch on, there's a possibility I could bluff my way through the gates before the alarm's sounded."

Bolan was unhooking his harness and holsters from the closet. "It's all right," she said, seeing him start to remove the Desert Eagle's magazine. "I know she changed them all for blanks, but I paid a visit to the armory when nobody was looking. They're both loaded with the real thing."

"Good girl," Bolan said. "How do we get to your car?"

She laid a finger to her lips and led him up a flight of stairs, through a double doorway and along a short passage. At the heavy double doors blocking off its farther end, she whispered, "There's a courtyard outside here, on the far side of the house to the burned-out stables. The car is just inside the gates."

He eased back the catch and inched open one of the doors. Gradually the hairline of daylight widened until he could peer through into the open air. The car—it was the Fiat sedan he'd seen in the garage at Latta's house in Belgium—was there all right, hidden from the house by a clump of overgrown rhododendrons. Beyond it was the high wall of a vegetable garden, and then the driveway leading past the front of the castle to the stableyard and the woods.

But between them and the sedan loomed the broad shoulders of a Maccione gunner. He was standing with his back to them, a mini-Uzi at the ready, staring through the gates toward the lake.

Katrina sketched a brief pantomime with one hand, motioned Bolan back out of sight then jerked the door noisily open. "Brockmann!" she called. "Here!"

The guard turned slowly around, his brutish face creasing into a frown. "What's the trouble?" he demanded suspiciously, approaching the door.

"It's the prisoner below," Katrina said agitatedly. "He's...come and look, please. Quick!"

The big guy snicked back the safety on his weapon, bent his head and strode through the doorway. Katrina was already at the top of the stair, beckoning.

Bolan had cached himself in the deep shadows behind the open door. As soon as the guard passed through, he stole up behind the man, poised on one leg and slammed his other heel down as hard as he could on the gunner's right hand and the butt of the Uzi's pistol grip protruding from the palm.

The SMG, knocked from his grasp by the impact, clattered on the floor as he whirled around with a snarl of rage.

Before the hardguy could shout an alarm, Bolan had danced in close, his forearm held across his chest, his fingers extended in a cobra strike, his flat hand darting out, axing the guard's throat.

The man staggered, grunting. He wasn't going to be able to cry for help for a while, but he was tough. The guy didn't fall. Choking, he rushed at the warrior with outstretched arms and seized him in a bear hug.

Bolan tried every fighting trick he knew. He butted the guy's nose with his forehead; he hacked his shin; he brought up a sharp knee. But the hardguy was immovable; wheezing, purple in the face, he merely increased the pressure. Inexorably the arms tightened around Bolan like steel bands.

The warrior's spine felt as though it were about to snap. His own arms, pinioned to his sides in that viselike embrace, were seized with cramps. It was when his senses were reeling that he resorted to the oldest trick of all. He went abruptly limp.

With a growl of satisfaction, the guard relaxed his grip enough to let Bolan slide down within his grasp. When his elbows were free, the warrior's bunched fists hammered with piston precision into the hardman's unprotected belly and savaged his diaphragm. All at once the rest of the Executioner was free....

The purple visage paled to a livid green, the remainder of his breath wheezed from tortured lungs, and the guard careened over against the wall and slid to the floor. At the same time Katrina slammed the side of his head with the butt of the subgun she'd picked up from the floor.

"I better tie him up."

She shook her head. "No time. They'll know you've got loose before he regains consciousness anyway. Come on. Every second counts."

They ran back to the outer doors. Bolan checked that the coast was clear, then led her out.

They were within five yards of the Fiat when footsteps crunched on the graveled driveway just outside the open gates. Bolan pulled the woman down, lightning fast, behind the rhododendrons. Crouching there between the leaves, they saw Latta and Alexandra sprinting toward the cellar doors.

"I just don't get it," the man was saying irritably. "I told her when I agreed she should take the first shift. The current was to be switched on, hard, after the first five minutes, and left that way for some considerable time on that initial session."

"Yes," Alexandra replied, "and it's five minutes or more since we heard even a groan. At one time I even thought I heard whispering!"

The double doors opened and closed behind them.

Katrina Holman was on her feet. Her face was white. "Damn," she muttered. "They must have been listening to the tape, live, all the time! We have about ten seconds before they see the guard and raise the alarm. Let's go!"

They were still several feet from the sedan when Campos, Foxy-face and DaSilva, accompanied by the meaty bulk of Maccione, walked into the area between the gates. The Mafia boss spotted them. "What the hell...?" he roared.

Foxy-face and the cold-eyed killer whipped out handguns almost before the words were out of his mouth. But Bolan and Katrina were already running away from the gates.

"Get them!" the chief mobster shouted. "But keep the guy alive!"

Shots cracked out behind the Executioner and his rescuer as the double doors burst open and Latta and Alexandra ran into the yard. For an instant the shooting stopped and there was a confused exchange between the two groups. By the time Maccione's rasping voice had restored order and issued commands, the fugitives had turned the corner of the building.

They were faced with a wildness of weed-grown ground enclosed on two sides by the blackened walls of the gutted stables, the restored rear wing straight ahead of them, and the ruined facade of the castle's rear elevation on their right. "Which way?" Bolan panted. "The new wing?"

"No. Every corner's covered by video cameras. We'll have to make the old part and hope for the best."

An arched doorway, half hidden behind a screen of neglected wisteria, stood ten yards away. The timbers of the door itself, bone-white with age and fissured through lack of use, were slightly ajar. "In here," Katrina said urgently. "The restorers haven't touched this part of the castle. Nobody's been in here for years."

"But won't they know—"

"Not at first. There are other doors. We'll find a way out on the other side."

Bolan reckoned she'd earned his trust after her performance with the guard, especially in view of what Latta and Alexandra had said. He nodded briefly and strode to the door, shouldering the weathered wood. Running footsteps were fast approaching the corner of the building behind them.

The door squealed open only a few more inches before it jammed on the stone flags of a passageway inside. He pushed Katrina through the gap and squeezed in after her.

She was already running for a staircase thick with dust. Outside, he heard Maccione's voice. "DaSilva, try the hole in the stable wall. We'll check out the doors in this wing.''

At the top of the stairs was a small empty room. Katrina pushed open a door, and they found themselves in a long gallery, lit by sunbeams slanting down through ocular windows high in the castle's front facade. Beneath the windows were dozens of glass-fronted showcases, filled with exotic tropical moths. Many had fallen from their transfixing pins and the bottoms of the cases were thick with shriveled thoraxes and dead wings. Stuffed birds were behind them, their bright plumage faded. Angry voices echoed now at the foot of the stairway behind the fugitives, and they heard the jammed door roughly forced open.

Katrina pushed past a curtained arch at the far end of the gallery and they ran through another unfurnished room. Bare shelves yawned on every wall; only a stack of nibbled books rose in the center of the floor, its dark crannies alive with nests of mice.

Stags' heads mounted on wooden shields, along with moth-eaten fox masks and the front half of a wild boar, its back white with dust, looked down from the walls of the upper hallway they passed through next. Twin staircases curved down to the castle's original main entrance below.

But voices echoed from one of the rooms off the lobby and behind them—probably from the gallery—came the hoarse hunting cry of Maccione. "This way! They've been through here. I can see footmarks in the dust!"

"We'll have to go up," Katrina whispered. "*This* way!"

"Yeah, but—"

"Don't worry. The place is enormous. There are half a dozen more staircases that lead down."

They dashed to the far side of the hallway, but not fast enough...

"Hey, look! Up on the second!" One of the hoods, crossing the lobby, had seen them. The chase was on.

Bolan ran into the hallway above, passed a stone chimneypiece over which generations of spiders had woven their webs into a shawl of lace...and stopped dead.

Beneath the sagging rafters of a lofty room, dozens, hundreds, battalions of tall, muscular, dark men, each holding a .44 Magnum Desert Eagle pistol, stared unbelievingly back at him.

He stood at the entrance to the Hall of Mirrors.

"Wait," Katrina whispered behind him. "There's only one way out the other end, I think I can find it. But it might—"

"Okay," he cut in. "You take it. I'll use this to hold them off."

Arched alcoves, each with its mirror, some with two installed in a V pointing inward or outward, covered the entire wall space of the huge gallery. And there were many others, singly, in pairs or in trios, each set in an arch identical to those framing the alcoves, slanting across the floor at various angles.

The effect was hallucinatory. Bolan saw images of himself full face, from the rear, in profile, advancing and receding beneath a multitude of arches each time he moved—an infinity of Executioners in diminishing perspectives as far as the eye could be fooled.

So cunningly were the reflecting surfaces arranged that sometimes, apparently face to face with himself, he found the image moving left when he moved right. At other times he was brought up short by a sheet of plain glass in a space between mirrors. He was halted by one of these when he heard a call off to one side. "All right, Bolan. Drop the gun or you're a dead man!"

He swung around. Fifty more Bolans swung with him. Bruno DaSilva was beneath the entrance arch, his Smith & Wesson Model 59 pointing directly at . . . what?

Mack Bolan, the flesh and blood one, was actually at that moment out of his direct line of vision. He raised his arm. Fifty Desert Eagles menaced the Mafia killer; fifty more pointed away from him, left, right. But which was the reality; which was the illusion?

"Don't say I didn't warn you," DaSilva grated. He pressed the trigger. The whip-crack of the shot was deafening in the great hall, reverberations batting from frame to frame of the juxtaposed mirrors. One of the Bolans vanished in an eruption of shattered glass. Huge shards separated and dropped to the floor, leaving an empty arch . . . and through it, framed three yards beyond, another Executioner staring away to the right.

DaSilva cursed. He advanced a couple of paces, the autoloader's muzzle questing like a snake's head from side to side. The warrior's image moved again. One, ten feet to DaSilva's right, was aiming straight for the killer's chest. He swung around and fired again, twice.

The 9 mm slugs starred a sheet of mirror into a thousand pieces. Beyond it was another, reflecting yet more Bolans. They were smiling.

DaSilva panicked. He began firing blind, at every facing image that he could see. His own image, wild-eyed, wreathed in cordite fumes, was now repeated in some of the mirrors. The crashing of broken glass played a jangling obbligato to the gunshot cannonade.

Bolan vanished.

DaSilva halted, panting. He stared anxiously around him. No Bolan, but no crumpled figure on the floor, either. No wounded warrior trying to writhe out of reach.

One shot remained in the S&W's magazine. A single fragment of glass separated itself from a savaged frame and tinkled to the floor. After that there was silence.

There was one spot, one single square of varnished wood in the center of the gallery, that wasn't reflected in any of the hundred mirrors in the hall. Bolan stood there, guided by Katrina, who had explored the secrets of the castle before.

Nothing moved. Motes of golden dust remained suspended in the sunbeams that slanted through windows high up under the roof. From the farther reaches of the vast building a chorus of voices shouted questions. Nearer, somewhere on the same floor, Maccione bellowed orders.

DaSilva cracked. He strode three paces forward, his feet crunching on broken glass. "Bolan!" he yelled, his voice rising to a note of near-hysteria. "You son of a bitch! Where the fuck are you? Come out and fight!"

Fifteen feet to his left, five arched frames formed a quarter of a circle. Mack Bolan stepped suddenly into the center of each. "You have your chance," he said quietly.

Snarling, the killer hesitated for one hundredth of a second, chose the central image as the target for his last shot, fired.

Model 59 and Desert Eagle erupted at the same time, speaking each with a deadly but slightly different voice. Before the double thunderclap was lost among the rafters, the central Bolan flew apart in myriad jagged slivers and collapsed like a smashed jigsaw puzzle to the floor. DaSilva took the Desert Eagle's bullet between the fourth and fifth rib on the right-hand side, spinning sideways with white splinters of bone puncturing the gory hole smashed in his chest. He was dead before he hit the floor.

Bolan, the real Bolan, stepped out of the right-hand frame—from which the glass had already been blasted some time before—with the smoking Magnum in his hand.

Maccione and his followers were near now, still shouting.

"This way, quick!" Katrina whispered from behind him. "There's a ladder up to the attic floor, and from there we can reach one of the turrets with a stairway that goes all the way down to the Tunnel of Love."

They ran from the gallery, leaving a hundred killers dead on a field of bloodstained glass.

23

There were five interconnected rooms in the attic. Bolan and Katrina Holman scrambled up the ladder into the third. It was, like most of those in this deserted part of the castle, empty. Skylights spattered with pigeon droppings filtered in enough light to show dusty floorboards, many of them eaten away by dry rot.

The fourth room was something else. Clearly it had been used as a junkroom by some previous owner, perhaps even the ringmaster who built the place, because it was stacked so high with ancient rejects that only a narrow twisting alley between piles of broken furniture, disused bedding and cracked tableware allowed a free passage to the far end. Bolan could see why the most recent inhabitants hadn't bothered to take it with them when they left.

Smashed musical instruments strewed a groundswell of crates and boxes stuffed with papers, framed daguerreotypes, suitcases green with mildew and chairs with the stuffing eaten by rats. At one end of the stack, a huge pipe organ without a keyboard buttressed a pile of Victorian toys; at the other, the hide and head of a skinned baboon hung over a three-legged rocking horse and the shell of a broken drum.

Dramatically the organ groaned out a wheezing chord.

Bolan stopped dead and pulled the woman down to a crouching position. He held his breath, eyes straining in the gloom. Something small—wood? metal?—shifted imperceptibly up ahead. Motes swirled in the sunbeam sloping through a skylight high above the organ.

Someone was there in the stack, someone who had leaned inadvertently on one of the organ pedals, someone moving enough to displace one of the relics and create an updraft of air.

Bolan laid a finger to his lips and motioned Katrina to stay where she was. Bent double, he stole back toward the entrance to the twisting alley, turning at right angles around an upended kitchen table so that he was able to get a fresh slant on the farther reaches of the junk room. The maneuver paid off.

Because there *was* movement, no doubt about it. Between the bamboo legs of a garden chair stacked on top of a steamer trunk...a flick, a disturbance in the static organization of all that detritus piled beneath the rafters. A movement at the limit of his field of vision.

Very slowly, he turned his head. He was certain this time: bobbing up and down behind a chest of drawers, the top of a man's head. A head covered in short red hair.

Foxy-face.

He was moving around on the far side of the stack, hoping to take them unawares from the rear.

Bolan placed a foot on a crate of moldering books and raised himself higher. The wood gave way under his weight with a splintering crash. As he pitched backward, the hardguy's head and shoulders jerked up into view above the chest of drawers, a malevolent expression on his pinched features.

Both men fired at once, the roar of Bolan's Desert Eagle drowning the sharper crack of the mafioso's Walther

PPK. Neither scored—Bolan because he was off balance, Foxy-face because he'd been taken by surprise. The head of a china doll shattered behind the Executioner; his own shot flew high, plowing into the paneling below the skylight.

But the exchange had pinpointed the fugitives' position for the killers searching the rest of the castle. Bolan heard scrambling feet from all sides, boots pounding on stairways, the yells of Maccione and his confederates.

He releathered the .44 and whipped out the Beretta. There were seven shots left in the bigger gun and he had no spare clips; at close quarters the 9 mm autoloader's extra firepower could be conclusive. "Run for the turret!" he called to Katrina. "I'll join you there."

Splinters of wood cracked away from the tabletop as Foxy-face, aiming for the sound of Bolan's voice, triggered a round his way. The warrior dared everything once more on the unexpected approach. He righted the table and leaped onto the top so that he could look down on the gunner's hiding place.

Foxy-face was on his hands and knees, diving from the shelter of the chest for an overstuffed settee. With the 93-R in 3-shot mode, Bolan drilled the guy through the calf and cored the faded upholstery with the next two rounds. The mobster flopped out from behind it, spurting blood, and Bolan finished the job with a single shot to the guy's head.

The warrior was up and running. The sudden explosive rasp of a submachine gun erupted from the distant end of the gallery, followed by two revolver shots and then a second kill-burst from the stuttergun. He heard the clatter of a heavy body falling, a smothered curse, footsteps receding.

Katrina and the Uzi?

She was white-faced. "They came up the main stairway," she said shakily. "Two of them. I . . . I decked the first, but the other got away."

"Nice work. You okay?" He flashed a glance at the landing as she nodded. Through the open doorway he saw two legs, two loafers pointed at the ceiling, a trace of blood still glinting as it sank into the dusty floorboards. Men were climbing up from below.

Katrina opened a narrow door that slanted across a corner behind a seven-foot stack of mildewing bed mattresses. "This way," she whispered.

The door slammed behind them. The turret was no more than twelve feet in diameter, with stone steps spiraling around a central core—six flights of sixteen stairs each, ninety-six in all with a half-landing and a door at each floor of the castle.

They were down one and a half stories before the top door was jerked open and shots echoed thunderously down the masonry shaft. Maccione or one of his heavies was attempting to wing them with ricochets. But although lead screeched off the rounded wall nothing lethal came near. Bolan loosed two rounds from the Beretta, and they raced on down, Katrina's penlight splashing curves of damp stone ahead of them as they took the steps three at a time.

There were no more shots from above, just the clatter of feet following at a discreet distance.

Light, dazzling and intense, flooded the turret as they approached the second-floor landing. Behind the suddenly opened door and the beefy silhouette of a gunslinging mafioso, Bolan saw the spectacled, narrow skull of Giordano, the Liège capo.

The warrior's reaction time was faster than the contraction of the hardguy's trigger finger.

A violent shove sent Katrina hurtling down the stairway past the door to sprawl against the stonework of the turret's outer wall. At the same time the Beretta bucked convulsively in Bolan's iron fist, choking a 3-blast deathstream toward the enemy gunners.

The beefy hardman's lower jaw sagged as he gazed disbelievingly at a pulped hand from which the heavy six-shot .45 had been blown away, at the twin rosettes bubbling scarlet from the waistline of his pale blue seersucker jacket. He sat down, hard, rolled onto his right side, twitched once, and never closed his eyes again. The one shot fired from his gun levered a foot-long splinter from the wooden floor.

Giordano was already safely out of sight behind the door, flat on his face and trembling. His spectacles had fallen off in his haste to quit the firing line, and lay beside the dead gunner.

Bolan squandered a single round from the 93-R to pulverize the thick lenses. For a fleeting moment, his lips twisted into a shadow of a grin. Nobody but himself would appreciate the irony of the situation...and it meant one man less behind them who could aim on target.

"You okay?" he whispered to Katrina. "I'm sorry, but—"

"Forget it," Katrina cut in. "A couple bruised forearms are a better bet any day than a bullet in the gut!"

A knife-edged rectangle of white marked the outline of the first-floor doorway as they ran on down. Bolan unleathered the Magnum and blasted a single skullbuster through the timbers as a warning. Simultaneously two shots crashed out from the far side of the door, leaving three thin light beams probing the darkness of the turret. The door wasn't opened.

At basement level, the stairway stopped. There was no door here, just a narrow oblong trapdoor set in the floor.

"Down to the waterway?" Bolan queried.

She nodded. The penlight beam was starting to fade. "A ladder, I think. It's where the workmen used to come down to fix the Tunnel of Love stuff."

He was already tugging at an iron ring bolted to one end of the trap. At different distances above them, movements, voices, the stealthy opening of doors indicated a concentration of Maccione's remaining forces. "Good thing they have to take us alive," Bolan observed, "otherwise they could just roll a grenade down and finish it."

His legs were braced as he fought to free the trap. Corded muscles stood out on his forearms and neck. At last, with a screech of metal, the trapdoor opened, tearing away at the same time from its rusted hinges.

Below was darkness, a sound of rushing water, a current of air carrying the dank odors of decay, and a vertical ladder plunging into the unknown.

"They'll figure they have us trapped now," Katrina said. "There's a stone shelf beside each of the canals down there, but the exits are all barred with iron grilles."

"How deep is the water?"

"Just deep enough to float the boats. Not more than waist-high, most places."

"And the other places?"

"Beneath the grilles, about seven feet."

"Okay. Let's go." Bolan helped her down the ladder. The pursuit—at least four men, he thought—was drawing closer: a stealthy shuffling somewhere in the turret above. He maneuvered the torn away trapdoor through the gap in the floor, supporting its weight on one arm, and made it down the ladder. "You're wise to the way this place works," he said. "Brief me, but make it fast."

"There was a museum once, beneath the entrance lobby. They boarded the boats there. The water is siphoned off from a stream that runs through the property and down into the lake. But the boats weren't carried along by the current. There was machinery that pulled them through a network of narrow canals on wires, and they ended up in a basin with a landing, near the old stables."

"Does the water flow back into the stream that way?"

"No. It runs through these grilles, beneath the driveway out front, and then past the maze. It runs into the stream there and makes the lake down a series of cascades."

"That's the way we'll go," Bolan decided. He zippered his two guns into the waterproof neoprene pouch at his waist and lowered himself into the stream. It was ice-cold, almost up to his armpits, and tugged strongly at his legs. Katrina sat on the shelf and slid, gasping, into the water. From above and behind them, a hoarse shout echoed in the turret. The mafiosi had spotted the open trapdoor.

Bolan grabbed the wooden rectangle and pulled it off the ledge. It splashed down beside him. "Lean on it, lift your feet and use it as a surfboard!"

Together, grabbing the leading edge of the trap with outstretched hands, they raised their legs from the floor of the tunnel and were swirled away into the dark beneath the arched brick roof.

Light blazed down through the opening above the ladder. A powerful spot beam lanced the blackness of the underground waterway, fingering the green-slimed walls, shimmering off the frothed surface of the current. "Get after them!" Maccione's voice yelled. "They can't be far! Get the spot down on that goddamn walkway!"

The dazzling beam dipped, fell, and then swung the Executioner's way as boots clanged on the iron ladder. But the improvised raft had nudged the wall and then eddied away around a curve in the tunnel before the first fusillade roared out behind them and slugs plowed harmlessly into the brickwork.

It was an eerie voyage. Floating past the wires, jigs and hanging frames from which rubber skeletons had once grinned and nameless monsters veiled in artificial spiderwebs thrilled nineteenth-century ladies into their escorts' embrace, Bolan watched over his shoulder the play of light signaling the very real dangers threatening him and the young woman with him.

The spotlight shifted from one dripping wall to another as the ancient tunnel twisted and turned among the castle foundations. The water hissed and gurgled beneath the walkways, sometimes on the left, sometimes on the right, occasionally beneath a crumbling miniature bridge. Over it all reverberated the cries and the footsteps of his pursuers.

Strange mission, he thought, kicking the raft away from an obstruction projecting from the wall: dead men were supposed to tell no tales, but Zulowski had a tale to tell—and because Bolan had the key to it, here he was, the hunter, forced to spend the second half of the operation running from the people it was his natural inclination to attack.

If he made it, the Mob would be attacked all right, and hit where it hurt most—smack in the center of the pocketbook. By then, too, if luck was with him, there would be less of them to register the shock.

The darkness ahead was paling. Around a sharp bend daylight flooded down through a grimed glass roof onto a landing platform. Rusting machinery—a winch with toothed gears, pulleys, some kind of overhead gantry—stood at one side of the stage. Campos, his shattered arm still in a sling, stood at the other with two hardmen holding submachine guns.

But before the calm surface of the basin in front of the stage, most of the water spilled to the left and gushed through three iron grilles set ten feet apart in the tunnel wall. "Swim under water?" Bolan murmured.

"No problem," Katrina whispered in his ear.

"Okay. Let the raft float on. Give the boys some target practice. Grab my ankle with one hand and follow me."

In the narrow confines of the tunnel, their voices had carried. As the makeshift raft floated out into the basin, the stutterguns opened fire with a deafening clamor.

But Bolan was already underwater. With Katrina clinging to him, he dived deep beneath the first of the iron grilles.

24

Blood was hammering behind Bolan's eyes and a band of steel had tightened around his chest before the total blackness of the submarine tunnel at last lightened to a distant greenish-gray.

The tug of the underwater current, rushing slightly downhill now, aided by the Executioner's own powerful strokes carried the fugitives beneath the castle's entrance driveway, under a terrace and out finally into an ornamental pond.

They broke surface between the leathery leaves of water lilies, gasping for life-giving air. Scouring the bottom of the basin, the current escaped through a sluice to rejoin the original stream, leapfrogging over stone steps hidden beneath the undergrowth down to the lake. Twenty yards away on the opposite side of the pond was the unkempt mass of yew that formed the old maze.

And below that was the weed-grown slope dropping to the boat house, the rotting jetty... and the possibility of freedom.

It was raining again, heavy drops pockmarking the water surface and pattering on the lily leaves. "We've got to make the lake," Bolan said, "but they'll be onto us the moment we climb out of this pond."

"The maze," Katrina panted, tossing the wet hair out of her eyes. "There's overgrown shrubbery and briars as high as your head all the way down to the waterside beyond it."

He stared at her.

"I've studied it. I know the plan. It hasn't been clipped for years, but you can still make out the old passages. We'll be through it in a flash, before they have time to surround it."

Bolan grinned suddenly. "Whatever you say, lady."

He studied the slope on the near side of the maze. She was right. The weeds there were waist-high, and they could certainly drop down beneath them and crawl, but the waving grass tops would chart their progress as clearly as if the slope were freshly mown. "Okay, you go first," he said. "I'll cover you." He lifted the neoprene pouch above the level of the water and took out the Beretta.

"The formula's simple enough," Katrina said. "First left, first right, first right again. Then left, right, right two more times and a final double left to exit. Okay?"

The warrior nodded. "Get going."

The stone coping that bordered the rectangular basin was hidden by the weeds. Bolan leaned his elbows on it, folded down the autoloader's front handgrip, and held the gun two-fisted, parting the stalks with the muzzle so that he could see the weathered facade of the castle. Campos and his two henchmen were climbing steps from an area. Giordano was leading three more men around from the stableyard. Latta stood in front of the open entrance doors with a bullhorn. Bolan had noticed that the laundryman was always somewhere safe in the background whenever there was a chance of a shooting war.

Over the hiss of falling rain, Bolan heard leaves rustle as the young woman scrambled out of the basin and made for the entrance to the maze. Campos and Giordano couldn't hear, but they could see. Latta's bullhorn erupted, and the other two mafiosi yelled orders. The SMGs spit fire.

But the Executioner was in there pitching, too. The range was less than three hundred feet. With three single shots he blew away Giordano's gunners, and a second lethal hail sent Campos and his thugs scuttling away. Before they could get it together and work out the odds, the warrior had pulled himself up out of the basin and made a defense tackle's dive for the yew hedge covering the entrance to the maze.

He landed on hands and knees among the untrodden grasses and heard Katrina's encouraging call from farther inside the living puzzle. Scrambling upright, he cat-footed past intruding branches of the ancient evergreen with the woman's instructions echoing in his ears. Left, right, right; left, right, right—that was one hell of a drill sergeant's marching order for a military man!

Her voice was calling softly from somewhere ahead. He turned through a gap in the closely packed yew. Was that the first left turn? No, one of the bushes forming the hedge had died. He was in a cul-de-sac, facing a lichened marble nymph on a pedestal. He hurried back to the main alley. Yeah, the real openings were wider, still recognizable although long strands of greenery trailed out from the dense green walls.

He made the first five turns in double time, no problem; missed the sixth because it was overgrown and found himself facing an alley with no exit; retraced his steps and got it right. Katrina's voice—barely audible over the pelting of the rain—appeared to be behind him now. He reckoned, making a hasty orientation from the position of the low clouds scurrying overhead, that the route she'd given him zigzagged mainly around the outer confines of the maze without ever penetrating to the center.

He guessed right. After two more turns he passed a thinner section of the yew buttress and realized that he could peer through and make out the huge briar thicket blanketing the slope between the maze and the boat house.

And the saturnine figure of the Liège capo, Giordano, standing ten feet away with a submachine gun he must have snatched from one of his fallen hardmen.

Thinking Bolan and his companion would be trapped inside the maze, Giordano was about to rake the whole width of the yew complex with a lethal burst. Without glasses, it was easier than trying to aim.

He started at the far corner, the stubby deathblaster shuddering in his grasp as the muzzle belched flame. The killstream was halfway to Bolan's position, spewing twigs, branches and leaves into the alley, when the Executioner dropped the guy with a single shot from the Desert Eagle.

Giordano was flung backward with a spreading scarlet buttonhole, and lay among crushed grasses whose bloodied stalks were soon washed clean by the rain.

Shouts from the remainder of the hoods were now dangerously near. Bolan made it to the exit and found that, as Katrina had said, it was concealed beneath a great arched tangle of briars.

From outside, this spiny wilderness looked to be an impenetrable barrier, but beneath the inextricable ten-foot crisscross of thorned bushes there was room to crawl. And the bare earth, screened from daylight as well as rain by the briar barrier, was dry and free of the undergrowth that choked the rest of the slope.

Katrina was already fifteen or twenty yards ahead, negotiating on hands and knees the broken stone of a shallow flight of steps that had once separated two terraces. Bolan bypassed a cracked and fallen urn and joined her.

From somewhere outside the thicket came a sudden staccato burst of automatic fire. And then a voice—Campos, the Executioner thought—yelling, "Come out, the two of you. We know you're in there somewhere. You've got two minutes before we spray the yew with gasoline and smoke you out."

By the time the ultimatum expired Bolan and Katrina, at the expense of a dozen deep scratches from the tougher thorns, had scuttled to the foot of the slope. Between the briars and the water's edge there was nothing but a strip of long grass.

Bolan motioned Katrina to stay out of sight while he made a brief recon. He wormed his way forward until he could see each way along the narrow, twisting surface of the lake. Eastward, a quarter of a mile distant, was the dam that had turned the valley of the Sûre River into a reservoir. On his right, where the lake gleamed dully between densely wooded banks, was the sector reserved for boating, fishermen and swimmers. The water was deserted today, but a small craft was visible between the rotted timbers of the castle boat house, an inflatable dinghy, with the blue-striped white fiberglass cowling of a 40 HP Couach outboard tilted up over the gray rubber stern.

"All systems go!" Bolan whispered to the girl hidden in the briar thicket. "Vector in on the boat house, rear entrance."

He lowered himself into the water, which was between three and four feet deep below the bank. Bent forward so that his head and shoulders wouldn't show above the grasses, he began wading slowly toward the boat house.

Over the drumming of rain on the sagging roof he could now hear a sharper crackling noise. He looked over his right shoulder and saw that the crumbling western wing of the castle was obscured by a pall of black smoke. Campos was carrying out his threat to burn down the maze.

Bolan didn't know whether century-old yew hedges would blaze up all that easily in a downpour, even with gasoline as a boost, but the smoke was dense and choking enough: after a very short time without any visible or audible reaction, the wounded capo would realize the birds had already flown. After that, there was only one way he and the remaining killers would come: downhill to the lake.

Okay, so speed was now the number-one priority, surpassing silence, security and concealment. He leaned forward into the lake water and made it to the boat house entrance with a fast crawl.

Half the shingled roof had fallen in, and the walls above the rotting piles were fissured where planks had fallen away. But the part of the old boardwalk jetty that was still under cover was firm enough. Firm enough to support a small cabin cruiser, shored up on stocks. Firm enough for one of the piers to be used as a hitching post for the rubber dinghy.

Firm enough to take the weight of Vito Maccione, standing with braced feet at the inner end, the Ingram MAC-10 subgun in his hands trained on the Executioner as he surfaced by the outboard.

"Welcome home, sucker. I've been expecting you," the Mafia boss growled.

"The line's been used before," Bolan replied. His mind was racing. Both his guns were back in the waterproof pouch, along with the remaining stun grenade. The MAC-10 carried a 30-round magazine, firing .45-caliber ACP skullbusters at a cyclic rate of more than one thousand per minute.

For a man up to his armpits in water, a test of strength with that combination would be playing, as Maccione implied, at sucker odds.

"Never mind the quality of the dialogue," the mafioso said. "The scenario's already written and there's only one more scene to be played. Stay right where you are—the hands out of the water and held away above the head, okay?—until Campos and the boys come to collect you. After that it's back to the castle, where you're going to tell us what we want to know. Only this time the interrogation will be, let's say, a bit more intense."

Bolan raised his hands. "Suppose I don't want the part?" he said, playing for time.

"Quit stalling. Where's that double-crossing bitch?"

"Right behind you," Bolan said.

"Don't mess with me, Bolan," Maccione snarled. "Who you think you are? This is a game between professionals and you lost out. Do you really figure I'm going to fall for the oldest trick in the book while you leap out the goddamn lake and slug me from behind? Jesus!"

Although his hands were held above his head, the Executioner contrived at the same time a resigned sigh and a shrug. In fact he wasn't bluffing.

The doorway through which Maccione must have entered was on the far side of the decrepit shed. But immediately behind him vertical timbers had rotted away from the boat house frame, and there was an eighteen-inch gap in the wall.

Katrina Holman stood in the gap.

"Just push," the warrior said quietly.

"Look, punk, I told you..." Maccione began. And then, warned perhaps by some fighter's sixth sense, an indrawn breath, a tiny movement behind him, he did start to swing around.

Too late. Katrina was through the gap with arms outstretched, hurling herself forward to shove the mafioso in the small of the back with all the force she could muster.

Caught off balance, Maccione tightened his trigger finger long enough to blow another ragged hole in the boat house roof, then he fell. He hit the water with a tremendous splash, the subgun spinning out of his hands.

The gun sank from sight; Maccione surfaced, gasping, on the crest of the minor tidal wave he caused.

Bolan was already plunging forward. Lake water swirled and heaved anew as the two men grappled beside the dinghy.

It was one to one now, and the odds were even in every sense. Bolan had the advantage in height, but Maccione was thicker, heavier, and equally muscular. A certain amount of the Executioner's tempered-steel resilience had also been sapped by the subterranean underwater escape so soon after his ordeal in the cellar.

For him, then, the combat had to be fast: he had to finish it while his strength held up, and before Campos and the others arrived.

Maccione's left hand raked across Bolan's face, the faceted stones ringed on his four meaty fingers scratching the warrior's cheek from jawline to ear. Bolan responded with a flat-handed blow to the throat, but the resistance of the chest-high water slowed his normal cobra-quick dart, and the mafioso was able to seize the wrist in a nerve grip that threatened to paralyze the Executioner's right arm.

Bolan was forced to the one position where Maccione would be strongest—close quarters. He surged in and brought up a knee, but again the water impeded the movement and the motion was reduced to a slow-motion take that Maccione avoided with a sideways twist. It was a twist, nevertheless, that allowed Bolan to break the wrist hold, and for a moment the two men traded ineffectual punches above the waterline with only bobbing heads and half submerged shoulders for targets. Then the warrior's foot slipped on the mud-silted bottom of the backwater and the very situation he fought to avoid was imposed on him. One of Maccione's gorilla arms encircled him just below the surface, pinioning his arms to his sides while the heel of the killer's other hand was jammed under Bolan's chin, forcing his head inexorably back into the water.

Katrina stood on the weathered wooden deck, a canoe paddle in her hands, but Maccione was out of reach of any blow she could land. She watched horror-struck as the capo leaned forward, increasing the pressure as first the back of the Executioner's head, then his ears and finally the eyes vanished beneath the muddy swell.

Bolan struggled with every ounce of his strength. In a moment his nose and mouth would be under. He kicked out furiously, hoping to knock Maccione off balance, but the man was standing foursquare with his feet planted wide. No way, that way.

Past the iron-hard grip choking the breath from his lungs, the warrior managed to breath in a last tortured gasp of air...and hold it. Then he was completely under. But to hold him there Maccione was leaning a long way forward from the waist now, his muscles bunched but his weight less well balanced.

Bolan relaxed the top half of his body, feigning a swimming away of consciousness and will. At the same time his legs shot out and scissored around the killer's calves while he twisted violently from the hips. And this time Maccione *was* taken by surprise.

His feet slid from beneath him and he floundered. Bolan freed his own legs, jackknifed the knees, and thrust forward both heels to slam into the killer's crotch.

Involuntarily Maccione doubled up with his mouth open. Bolan's linked hands were there to force him facedown beneath the surface, where muscular spasm sucked a choking mouthful of water into his lungs. He jerked back, chest heaving, with water cascading from his agonized face. But Bolan, half out already, leaped forward, rammed his hands on the edge of the deck, and used his feet to kick Maccione back underwater.

With the deck as leverage, he hoisted himself up and thrust down hard on the hood, keeping him not only below the surface but shoving him between two pilings beneath the deck.

The water threshed and bubbled. Despairing gurgles percolated through the splash and slap of wavelets against the underside of the deck. Hands scrabbled desperately at Bolan's legs, nails tore his calves. But he maintained the pressure with furrowed brows, teeth gritted and every muscle tensed until the movements slackened and finally ceased.

Maccione floated out from beneath the deck, the muddied shantung suit stained with blood from the Executioner's split cheek. The scarlet splotches diluted, faded and then washed away as Katrina jerked the dinghy's outboard into life.

Bolan folded himself aboard and unzippered the neoprene pouch; the craft surged forward from beneath the boat house roof. They hit the open water as Campos and three hard-faced gunners made the grassy bank.

Katrina banged the throttle open wide and the dinghy squatted low in the lake and screamed away with the outboard roaring.

Campos opened fire first, shooting an old .38-caliber Police Special with his undamaged hand. He could have left the cylinder unturned, for the range was well over one hundred yards and increasing every second. The hardguys were something else. They were equipped with full-size Uzis—effective range, according to specification, two hundred meters.

One of the killers fired from the hip, the other two dropped to their knees among the grasses and traded a slightly longer range for a firmer stance. Bolan pushed the young woman to the floor and swung the craft's tiller left and right as he unleathered the Desert Eagle. For a few seconds the wooded lakeside echoed to the clamor of multiple automatic fire.

The guy who tried to get in first by firing from the hip paid for his impatience with his life: Bolan's first shot blew him away and he toppled into the water with half his face missing. The killstream from the others was more accurate: while flame belched from the Uzi muzzles, lethal hornets zipped past the wildly zigzagging dinghy. A slug nicked the lobe of the Executioner's ear, spraying his jacket with blood. Another sliced open the breast pocket of his jacket and tore away the button. Katrina gasped and put up one hand as a bullet parted the hair on top of her head without touching the scalp.

Exhausting the Desert Eagle's magazine one-handed, Bolan saw that he had scored a second time, bowling one of the remaining Uzi men over on his back with a smashed shoulder. The guy lay thrashing in the grass and screaming while Campos yelled at his companion to fire faster. The warrior pulled the Beretta out of the neoprene pouch.

But the dinghy was already out of range, heading fast for a bend where the lake curved around a spur in the hillside.

"Latta, Campos and at least one other gunner are still operational," Bolan said, shoving the 93-R back in his shoulder rig. "Is there any way they could cut us off by car?"

"There's a road," Katrina told him, "but they'd have to go back to Esch and then all the way around the hills via Boulade. And the lakehead's only a couple miles from the Belgian border." She shrugged. "By the time they made it back up to the castle..."

But they didn't make the lakehead. Several 9 mm punctures were letting air escape from the rubber stern, and although the bulging bulkheads were compartmented, the dinghy gradually lost speed as it settled lower in the water. They had to swim the final two hundred yards and then make it to the border on foot.

As they waded ashore Bolan saw the firestreak of missiles above a forest ridge ahead, and then heard the crump of exploding warheads. Seconds later flame blossomed among the trees and a shattering concussion threw rock fragments and splintered branches high into the air.

"Artillery!" he exclaimed, staring at the brown smoke boiling up into the rain. "Don't tell me Maccione is that sophisticated!"

Katrina laughed. "Don't you read the papers? This is Operation Breakthrough, the big NATO war games exercise replaying the Nazi attack at Sedan in 1940 with modern high-tech equipment."

"Of course." Bolan remembered the army convoys he'd seen on the Belgian expressway, the truck he'd climbed aboard to escape from Liège. He saw the red Restricted Area warning notices with their white skull-and-crossbones motifs at the water's edge. Dun-colored vehicles maneuvered among the trees higher up the hillside.

"As an armed civilian with no papers," Katrina began, "I'd like to know how you plan to make it across that territory and contact your own people without being arrested as an Eastern Bloc agent spying on the operation."

"No problem," the Executioner replied. "I borrowed an army command car a few days ago. If I haven't lost the technique, I could do it again."

"M-m-make it f-f-fast if you c-can," she said, shivering. "I've never been so cold in my l-life!"

He took in her rain-drenched hair, the sodden clothes that clung to her body and stripped off his jacket to drape over her shoulders.

It was then, noticing the ripped pocket and the missing button, that he took out the vital shades for which he had risked so much.

The slug that missed the warrior's heart and carried away the button had in fact scored a second and more valuable bull's eye.

In its trajectory, it had passed through an eyepiece of the Zulowski sunglasses and shattered forever the remaining lens of the damaged pair.

EPILOGUE

"According to this official complaint from State," Hal Brognola said severely, "making off with that goddamn command car cost Blue Army an entire division in the war games."

"That's too bad," Bolan replied. "But—"

"And Blue Army is us, which makes it worse. It seems, looking for a place where you could make your damned transmission uninterrupted, that you crossed into Red Army territory, and the games umpires—"

"There's just one thing, Hal," Bolan cut in. "You and me, we're not playing games. Right?"

"Okay, okay." Brognola sighed. "It's just that...well, if it wasn't for the fact that this is the second time..." He shook his head resignedly. "And all for a pair of smashed spectacles as useless as the original holograms Zulowski sent!"

The phone on Frank O'Reilly's desk rang. He picked it up. "Security," he said. "Yeah?...Right away?...Okay, wilco." He turned to the Fed. "Mr. Brognola, they'd like to see you in the lab. The chief tech says he has news for you."

Brognola levered himself to his feet. "Okay," he said to the Executioner, "now for the bad news."

Upstairs in the small second floor, white-coated assistants were setting up apparatus on a bench. Bolan saw a helium-neon laser similar to the one demonstrated at the NATO research station by Colonel Heller. Beyond it was a hologram plate in a movable clamp—and between them, in a complicated cradle of adjustable jaws, the battered shades he'd gone through so much to bring home.

"A million to one, I'd say," Bolan mused, staring at the chipped sidepieces, the one empty frame and the splintered lozenge of tinted glass in the other. "A lens cracked and starred like that couldn't pass light through the same way an undamaged one would, could it?"

"You're worrying needlessly, sir," the chief tech said. "We carried out a few experiments before we called you. Just watch." He turned a switch and plunged the room into darkness.

A pink glow suffused the bench as the laser hummed into life. Rose-colored fingers manipulated the clamps, maneuvering the sunglasses this way and that...and suddenly, as astonishingly as a conjuror producing huge flags from an empty hat, the meaningless specks on the hologram plate vanished and they saw floating in three dimensions before them a sheet of paper covered from margin to margin in single-spaced typescript.

The report listing members-designate of the Mob's master plan for Europe had been decoded at last!

"It was the *starred* lens Zulowski had used all the time, you see," the chief tech explained. "I guess it was the nearest he could get, optically, to frosted glass in the time he had. The plain, undamaged lens had nothing to do with his hologram!"

"I'll tell you one thing," Brognola said grimly. He snatched up a phone, punched out a three-digit number. "Frank? Send a photographer up to the optics lab at once. Holography may be a high-tech marvel, but glass plates can get broken as easy as sunglasses, and I'm holding my breath until this report's enshrined in a roll of good old-fashioned 35mm ASA 100 stock!"

He turned to the Executioner. "Once that's done, maybe we can get around to that backpacking. I guess you could use a couple hours of relaxation now that the mission's successfully terminated?"

"Terminated?" Bolan echoed. "Latta, Campos and Alexandra Tauber are still at large. We still have to identify and round up the four people who penetrated the security of this safehouse when they grabbed me. The killers who knocked off Alexiou, Whetnall and the woman witness have to be convicted. Lieutenant Benito tells me he has a line on the character who rented the private plane that flew me to Europe. Hal," he said, "this operation only just *started*!"

Nile Barrabas's most daring mission is about to begin . . .

THE BARRABAS BLITZ

JACK HILD

An explosive situation is turned over to a crack commando squad led by Nile Barrabas when a fanatical organization jeopardizes the NATO alliance by fueling public unrest and implicating the United States and Russia in a series of chemical spills.

Out of the ruins of civilization emerges...

DEATHLANDS

The Deathlands saga—edge-of-the-seat adventure not to be missed!

Quantity

PILGRIMAGE TO HELL became a harrowing journey high in the mountains. — $3.95 — ☐

RED HOLOCAUST brought the survivors to the freakish wasteland in Alaska. — $2.95 — ☐

NEUTRON SOLSTICE followed the group through the reeking swampland that was once the Mississippi Basin. — $2.95 — ☐

CRATER LAKE introduces the survivors to a crazed world more terrifying than their own. — $2.95 — ☐

HOMEWARD BOUND brings the journey full circle when Ryan Cawdor meets the remnants of his own family—brutal murderers. — $3.50 — ☐

PONY SOLDIERS introduces the survivors to a specter from the past—General Custer. — $3.95 — ☐

Total Amount — $ _____
Plus 75¢ Postage — .75
Payment enclosed — _____

TAKE 'EM NOW

FOLDING SUNGLASSES FROM GOLD EAGLE

Mean up your act with these tough, street-smart shades. Practical, too, because they fold 3 times into a handy, zip-up polyurethane pouch that fits neatly into your pocket. Rugged metal frame. Scratch-resistant acrylic lenses. Best of all, they can be yours for only $6.99.

MAIL YOUR ORDER TODAY.

Send your name, address, and zip code, along with a check or money order for just $6.99 + .75¢ for postage and handling (for a total of $7.74) payable to Gold Eagle Reader Service. (New York and Iowa residents please add applicable sales tax.)

Remove from pouch...

unfold once...

unfold twice...

and they're ready to wear.

Gold Eagle Reader Service
901 Fuhrmann Blvd.
P.O. Box 1396
Buffalo, N.Y. 14240-1396

GES-1A

Offer not available in Canada.